Doug wondered what his problem was

He was twenty-nine; he was single; up until now he had always considered his sexual appetite to be healthy.

You're in deep trouble, Lacayo, he told himself. You've become fixated on an underage student who stole your clothes and makes a fool out of you in class.

He was very close to crossing over the line from normal behavior to aberrant behavior. He was very close to committing a crime. After twenty-nine years of clean living, he had to actually fight off the urge to walk into the school office and look up her address.

It wasn't really his fault, of course. *He* hadn't started it. She'd been coming on to him since her first day in class. Girls like that shouldn't be allowed in high school.

What the hell was she up to?

ABOUT THE AUTHOR

Beverly Sommers recently moved to an apartment on East Sixty-third Street in Manhattan, which she is decorating as a Mexican café. Readers visiting New York can feel free to stop by for a taco.

Books by Beverly Sommers

HARLEQUIN AMERICAN ROMANCE

HARLEQUIN INTRIGUE

Don't miss any of our special offers. Write to us at the following address for information on our newest releases.

Harlequin Reader Service
901 Fuhrmann Blvd., P.O. Box 1397, Buffalo, NY 14240
Canadian address: P.O. Box 603,
Fort Erie, Ont. L2A 5X3

OUTSIDE IN

BEVERLY SOMMERS

Harlequin Books

TORONTO • NEW YORK • LONDON
AMSTERDAM • PARIS • SYDNEY • HAMBURG
STOCKHOLM • ATHENS • TOKYO • MILAN

This is for Jill Wyckoff,
my only relative who actually
buys my books and reads them.
Thanks, Jill.

Published February 1990

First printing December 1989

ISBN 0-373-16331-2

Prologue

Overhead a jet was banking over the water before heading due north. The night was warm, still in the seventies, the humidity way up there. A strong wind was blowing in off the ocean and causing the palm trees to sway seductively in rhythm to the lapping of the waves on the shore.

In the shadow of the pier, Ernesto was setting up for the night. When he thought about it at all, he deemed himself lucky to be homeless in South Florida rather than in the north where the elements would likely as not kill him some night. Right now, though, all he was thinking about was the bottle of wine he had scrounged up the money for and the cigarette butts he had found in a parking lot where someone had dumped out a car ashtray. It was almost enough to persuade him that he was homeless from choice, that he chose to live on the beach and sleep under the stars, that he didn't miss the dead-end job and the room he had shared with a boiler and his weekly dominoes games at the neighborhood *bodega* with his friend, Felipe, who was always good for a couple of bucks when he needed it.

He stretched out the beach towel with the picture of an alligator on it that he had found abandoned in the sand one day and used now as a bed. He didn't mind the sand, but the sand fleas were fierce this year and the towel offered the illusion of protection.

He took the cigarette butts out of his pockets and lined them up in front of him on the back of the alligator. They averaged about half filters and half nonfilters and he picked up the nonfilters and buried them in the sand because they were already smoked right down to the cardboard. He chose one of the longer butts and lit it, then unscrewed the top of the bottle of cheap wine and held it up a moment, as though appraising it, before lifting it to his mouth and taking the first satisfying swallow. It went down warm and mellow and he tried to appreciate it while he could because soon he would be beyond even knowing what he was drinking, or caring.

After two drinks he always thought he could see Cuba on the horizon, beckoning him, luring him into the ocean for the long swim. But there was nothing for him there now, except maybe jail. And if he had his choice he'd choose jail in the States to jail in Cuba. He'd spent a few nights in jail for drunk and disorderly and a couple of times for vagrancy, and the cot had been soft and the food had been warm and he'd been half-reluctant to leave in the morning.

He preferred his place under the pier; it was beginning to feel like home. It was early yet, the sun not yet down, but later there would be others who would join him. There might be some food and more wine to share. A few nights ago, or maybe it was a few weeks, there had even been a cigar for him to enjoy. He still thought about that cigar in odd moments.

Ernesto heard their laughter before he saw them. He knew at once that it wasn't anyone he knew. The others didn't laugh like that, not with pleasure, not with that youthful tone that said life was still wondrous. He looked around and saw three young men walking across the sand in his direction. They looked as if they had just stepped out of a television commercial, with their skin bronzed by the setting sun and their muscular bodies set off by the briefest of swimming trunks. One of them carried a bat and the others baseball gloves. The ones with the gloves were tossing a ball back and forth as they walked, their arms graceful and glinting in the last of the light.

As they got closer he could see they they weren't young men at all but still boys, maybe sixteen, seventeen. They were tall and well built, but their faces didn't look as though they'd seen a razor, and their laughter was that of children. Two of them were dark and one had tight blond curls and all of them were quite beautiful in the way that youth and health and spirit are always beautiful.

He was so used to feeling invisible, of people's eyes passing right through him on the street, that he was surprised when they didn't walk right by him. Instead they stopped a few feet away, and smiles spread across their faces like warm margarine across Cuban bread.

"Hey, you want to play some ball?" one of the dark ones asked him, still smiling.

Ernesto pointed to his foot, the one with the sore that wouldn't heal and that caused his foot to swell to twice its size.

"Will you look at that?" said the blond boy, squatting down to take a close look at his foot. "It looks like a balloon about to pop, doesn't it? I'll bet if you stuck a pin in it it would explode."

The one with the baseball bat moved in for a look, but instead of a look he swung the bat down on Ernesto's foot, causing him to let out a scream of pain fierce enough to wake the night.

"You were wrong, it didn't pop," said the boy with the bat. The others found this funny and staggered around, slapping each other on the back.

The pain seemed to be flowing upward from his foot, and Ernesto took a long drink of the wine, trying to numb it. He didn't even question why the boy had hit his foot with the bat. He had long ago lost any sense of having any control over what happened to him.

The blond boy grabbed the bottle of wine from out of Ernesto's hand and started to lift it to his mouth.

"Hey, don't even think about it," one of the others said to him. "This guy could have any disease you could name."

Showing off his strong arm, the blond hurled the bottle like a curve ball so that it landed in the ocean and disappeared. Ernesto felt the tears then, not for his foot, which was still throbbing, but for the loss of the anesthetic that had been so casually tossed away.

"Look at all those cigarette butts," said one of the boys. "That's disgusting. Hey, old man, don't you know that smoking can kill you?" There was more laughter as Ernesto quickly reached for the butts and stuffed them back in his pockets.

"Okay, what's the batting order for tonight?" asked the blond, and for a few moments Ernesto thought they were going to go back to their game and leave him alone.

"I feel a hitting streak coming on," said the boy with the bat.

"Hey, you were first last time," said the other dark-haired one, making a grab for the bat, but the boy holding it pulled it away in time.

"I don't mind hitting clean-up," said the blond.

"All right, go ahead, give it your best shot," said the boy with the glove.

The batter hefted the bat and took a few practice swings. Just as Ernesto was waiting for the other boy to throw him the ball, a memory surfaced. Other homeless men he had heard about, beaten to death on the beach. But he shook his head, not believing it, and so did not see the first blow that was aimed straight at his head.

Overhead a jet was banking over the water before heading due north.

Chapter One

It was a moment of pure terror; the kind of moment nightmares are made of. Jill froze, unable to utter a word as all heads in the classroom turned in her direction.

It was a simple algebra problem, something that wouldn't have given her a moment's trouble when she was in high school. But now, ten years later, it looked like Greek to her.

"Jill, you want to give it a try?" asked the teacher, a man in his early fifties with curly gray hair and sympathetic eyes. It seemed that he was aware of her terror and was trying to give her a way out.

She kept asking herself why she cared, why she was afraid. Lightning wasn't going to come down and strike her because she couldn't remember algebra. It didn't even matter if she flunked the course. Then why was she suddenly feeling the old fear of being called on in class when she wasn't prepared? Hadn't she outgrown that by now?

Jill shook her head, lowering her eyes and trying to look the very picture of the shy, new girl in school. There was some sniggering from the boys, but Mr.

Colwin quickly called on someone else to go to the board and the class got back to normal.

So far she seemed to be striking out.

Strike one: she was dressed completely wrong. Had kids stopped wearing jeans to school or did fashions in South Florida differ that radically from northern Michigan? A few of the boys wore jeans, but most of them wore baggy shorts. And all the girls wore miniskirts. Plus the backpack she had slung over her shoulder for her books might be what the boys used, but all the girls had straw bags with leather handles. If she had wanted to stand out she couldn't have planned it more perfectly. The trouble was, she wanted to blend in.

Strike two: she drove into the high school parking lot that morning in a borrowed Honda Civic, and not a very new one at that. With the exception of a few moderately priced cars that were parked in spaces reserved for teachers, every other car in the lot was a Mercedes, a BMW or a Porsche. Kids actually turned to look at her car, that's what an anomaly it was. She immediately felt like a poor country cousin.

Strike three: whatever made her think that high school subjects would be a breeze? The fact that she had a graduate degree from Michigan State? The fact that she had above-average intelligence? The fact that she had made straight As in high school? Forget it! If she ever knew algebra, it was sure failing her now. She'd be lucky if she could do fifth-grade fractions anymore.

Plus the shock of being back in a classroom situation was unnerving. Only days ago she had been at a distribution point in Dire Dawa, apportioning the food to be sent to the different stations; now she was sitting in a high school algebra class feeling like the class dunce. It was the closest thing to going back in time she was ever likely to experience.

She closed her eyes for a moment and pictured herself back under the hot African sun that never seemed to make shadows. Birds would be circling overhead, somehow knowing there was food in the area. Laborers in white would be loading up camel caravans that would travel to Harar and Jijiga and as far as Dagabar.

Jill lifted her head and caught three blond cheerleader types two rows ahead looking her over. She had worried that at age twenty-seven she might not be able to pass for seventeen, but these girls calmed that worry. With their masses of stiffly moussed hair, their layers of eye makeup, their sexy little skirts and body-hugging tank tops with the bodies to fill them, they would have been able to breeze into any bar and consume a couple of drinks while she'd still be standing at the entrance getting carded.

For the most part, the students looked cloned. The girls practically all had masses of blond hair; the boys almost all had dark hair. From this she could only deduce that most of the blondes weren't natural since she didn't believe that blond parents only had girls and brunette parents boys. Hers was naturally blond, but she didn't seem to have enough of it for this school. Most of the boys had longer hair than hers. In fact the only thing she seemed to have in common with the girls was her tan. And that wasn't from sunbathing on the beach.

Jill opened her notebook and wrote a note to herself: LEARN ALGEBRA!!!! She underlined it several times. She'd need to do some extensive studying for a while in order to catch up, that was all. Soon it should all start coming back to her. At least next period was senior civics, which meant current affairs, and if she didn't know more about that than these kids, she'd give it up. She read the newspaper every day now, which was more than she ever did in high school. On the other hand, there was a new president she knew nothing about and God knows what else she'd missed out on since she'd been away.

Jill saw the one other out-of-place girl looking over at her with kind eyes. She had already noticed her in home room. She didn't fit in with all the beach bunnies, but she probably wouldn't fit in at any high school. She was fat. Her pink skirt came down to her chubby knees; her bra straps kept straying from beneath the shoulders of her oversized tank top; and, unfortunately, her hair was that orangy shade of red and resembled a Brillo pad. She was also dead white in a sea of richly tanned bodies.

Jill felt the girl would have survived better in her old high school in Michigan where at least she could have covered her body in thick clothes in the winter and not worried about burning that white, freckled skin. She probably still wouldn't be popular, but at least she wouldn't look quite so out of place.

When the bell rang, Mr. Colwin stopped Jill on her way out of class.

"Sorry about that. I guess I panicked," she said, and at his look of surprise realized, belatedly, that she had spoken to him as an equal. She quickly rearranged her features and modified her voice. "I need to catch up a little," she said with lowered eyes.

"Is the class too advanced for you?" he asked her.

"Oh, no," Jill lied, "it isn't that. It's being in a strange school, in a strange country. There were only two other students in my class in Ethiopia."

"That must have been fascinating," said Mr. Colwin. "You just take your time getting used to things, Jill. When you're ready to be called on, just raise your hand."

She thanked him and hurried out into the hall to find her next class. *When she was ready to be called on?* She didn't think she'd ever be ready in that class. In fact, what she had thought was such a great idea was turning out to be just as futile as her mother said it might be, although for different reasons.

Jill instantly felt remorse at the thought. Her sister was dead and she was worried about a little heat on her in algebra. She should be willing to get up in front of the class and make a fool of herself ten thousand times if it would help her to find out what happened to Susan. And that, after all, was her only reason for being here. Anything less would not have served as incentive enough to leave Africa where she was needed.

She arrived at civics just as the bell was ringing. There were only two remaining seats in the class: in the last row—in the midst of what was certain to be jocks—and in the front row. Ten years ago she would have taken the front seat without a thought. For one thing, she had never been the type of student who minded being called on. For another, there was no way during her high school years that she would have been the only girl sitting with the jocks.

Now she headed straight for the back, ignoring the looks of surprise she was getting from all sides. The jocks blatantly looked her over as she slid into the desk and took out her notebook. She was pleased to find she couldn't care less. There was no way high school boys had the power to intimidate her anymore. Maybe she looked the shy daughter of missionaries that she was supposed to be, but underneath the pose she was ten years older than these bozos and could no doubt teach them a thing or two.

In fact she was feeling so brave that she looked over at the boy on her right and gave him a smile. She could swear he started blushing, but he was so tan it was hard to be sure. She was just starting to think that some of these high school boys were pretty cute, when she heard a stir and saw the teacher take his place at the front of the room.

He did two simple things: he said good-morning and he smiled at the class, and all of a sudden she was thinking, *What do we have here?* He was so damn appealing that the cute boy next to her was reduced to the ordinary high school jock that he was. On the other hand, maybe she had just been out of the country too long.

Get hold of yourself, she warned her body, which was suddenly stirring in unseemly ways. The entire purpose of this class, of this whole charade, was to meet the boy in civics with whom Susan had fallen in love. The purpose was not for her to get her hormones in an uproar over the first sexy man she'd seen in three years.

Nor was she the kind of brainless person who took instant attractions seriously. But her body didn't seem to know that.

He was taking roll call and it was a good thing that Wyckoff was the last name called because it gave her time to calm down and get serious. A crush on a teacher? Ridiculous. She wasn't a teenager anymore.

When he finally got to her name and she called out, "Here," he looked up and located her in the back row.

"Welcome," he said to her, and she could hear the jock next to her mutter, "Yeah, welcome."

Jill nodded, forcing her eyes down and away from the teacher's face.

"You're new, right?"

"Right," mumbled Jill.

"Where'd you transfer from?" he was asking her.

"Out of the country," she muttered.

"I'm sorry, could you speak up?"

Jill looked up and felt like a butterfly being pinned by his dark eyes. "I was going to school in Ethiopia," she said, and several of the students started to laugh.

"Is there something funny about Ethiopia?" asked Mr. Lacayo, looking around the class.

The laughter stopped.

"No, I'd really like to know what's funny about that," he said.

The kids didn't seem afraid of him. One of the boys spoke up, asking, "Isn't that where all those people are starving to death? Didn't they do a rock concert for them or something?"

"That's right," said Mr. Lacayo. "Is that what you find funny? People starving to death?"

One of the girls said, "Boys always laugh at everything. They don't know what they're doing."

This got a few more laughs and it also got Jill off the hook with the teacher because he started in on the question of why people laugh at things that make them uncomfortable.

The guy next to her, the one she had smiled at, whispered, "You don't look African."

"You don't look stupid," she told him, with her sweetest smile. This got a laugh from some of his buddies. It also caught Mr. Lacayo's attention.

"Did you want to add something, David?" Mr. Lacayo asked him.

The blond Adonis to Jill's right slid down in his desk and tried unsuccessfully to hide from the teacher.

Then Mr. Lacayo turned the full warmth of his smile on Jill. "You might feel more comfortable up here in the first row," he said to her, and this time it was the girls who were laughing.

But not even his smile was going to sucker her into moving to the front row. She didn't think kids were any judges of age, but Lacayo didn't look much older than she did and she wasn't going to take any chances.

"I feel at home back here," she said, "Like being back in the bush," which wasn't at all the kind of thing she ever would have said at seventeen, but at twenty-seven she suddenly didn't give a damn.

There was more laughter and some approving looks from the students, and Jill felt it went a little way in undoing the disastrous first impression she must have made.

"Which just goes to prove there's no accounting for taste," said Mr. Lacayo. Then he launched into the subject of the day: the latest crisis in Central America.

Maybe six students in the class knew what he was talking about; maybe two students cared. Jill both knew and cared, but she had shown off enough for one class. Anyway, she was perfectly happy just looking at Mr. Lacayo.

He was dressed the way she was used to people dressing, in jeans and a T-shirt and an old, tan corduroy jacket. He looked more Michigan State than Palm Cove High School. In Africa, of course, he would have left off the jacket. But then Africa wasn't air-conditioned the way this school was.

He had thick, dark hair cut short in the front but coming down over his jacket collar in the back. He was as dark as she was and she had been baked by a hot African sun. His brown eyes held both intelligence and humor, a combination she approved of. His nose just missed being perfect by having a bump in it and his mouth could only be described as generous. Well, not only. She guessed sexy would be just as good an adjective. She judged him to be about six feet, maybe 165 pounds, and he seemed to be in perfect condition. Her little sister sure hadn't taken after her if she could be interested in a high school boy with Mr. Lacayo in the same room.

"What's the real problem down there?" Mr. Lacayo was asking.

The class seemed to like him and there were several answers called out.

"Yeah, the military's a problem," said Mr. Lacayo, "and so are the drugs. And dictators aren't ever great to have around. But what's the real problem? What is it, underlying everything, that makes the situation so hopeless?"

"Poverty," Jill found herself saying, and got an answering smile from Mr. Lacayo.

"Exactly," he said. "I guess you learned something about that in Africa."

Jill didn't answer, just bent her head down to her notebook as he got a discussion going on economics.

"How poor is it in Ethiopia?" he asked her.

She tried to remember that she wasn't supposed to be an authority; as a student in Africa she wouldn't be expected to know too much.

"Very poor," she said.

Mr. Lacayo seemed to expect more of her. "Parts of Miami are very poor. Can you be a little more descriptive?"

Everyone was looking at her now and she thought if she were a teacher, she wouldn't pick on a new student that way. "Palm Cove looks very rich to me," said Jill.

"It looks that way to me, too," said the teacher, smiling around the classroom.

"Well, as rich as Palm Cove is," said Jill, "Ethiopia's even poorer."

"Keep going," said Mr. Lacayo.

Jill took a deep breath. "Okay. Say you bulldozed everything in Palm Cove. Everything. Every tree, every plant. And then the locusts moved in and ate every blade of grass. And then you took away all the food and all the water. And then you made it impossible for anyone to work and no way to get out of here. And then you went a whole year without any rain. Most of the people would be dead by then and the rest would be dying of starvation. That's almost how poor it is in Ethiopia."

"How do you like Palm Cove so far?" he asked her.

"Not very much."

"Why not?"

"It makes me feel guilty."

His eyes locked on hers for a long moment until she thought he could look into her soul. Then he broke eye contact, shook his head a little and continued with Ecuador.

She'd been a little too heavy for most of the class and they were avoiding looking at her now. All except for a dark-haired boy sitting two desks over from her. He seemed to be silently appraising her and even her scowl didn't make him desist. He probably thought she was a freak. Teenagers weren't supposed to worry about things like that. Well, maybe rich teenagers in Palm

Cove never gave any thought to poverty, but she bet poor teenagers did.

Near the end of the class Mr. Lacayo wound up the session on Central America and asked, "Did any of you guys read the Sunday paper?"

Most of the hands went up.

He looked back at the last row and said, "I'm not talking about the sports section, guys, or what's playing at the movies. I'm talking about the front page."

Most of the hands went down.

"Come on, let's hear it. What happened in our own beautiful, peaceful Palm Cove this weekend that made the front page?"

One of the girls said, "You mean the murder?"

"That's exactly what I mean," said Mr. Lacayo. "And who was murdered?"

"Some bum," said one of the boys, and there were a couple of snorts of laughter.

"It's the same story, isn't it?" asked the teacher. "It's poverty again. Do you think the police department of Palm Cove will investigate very thoroughly when it's only a homeless person on the beach who's been killed?"

Jill could see the kids trying to look concerned to please their teacher, but she could also see that underneath this pose was the kind of uncaring attitude that Mr. Lacayo was talking about. She had read the article, and the most shocking thing about it had been that it was the seventh derelict found beaten to death on the beach in as many months. It didn't seem to make sense for something like that to be happening in rich, law-abiding Palm Cove.

The bell rang, and as the kids started heading for the door, Mr. Lacayo yelled out, "Hey, gang, do me a favor and read the paper tonight."

She was hoping to go out unnoticed but Mr. Lacayo's voice stopped her. "Jill? Do you have a moment?"

She turned back, letting the last of the jocks file out past her. One of them said, "Uh-oh," and winked at her on the way out.

"Yes?" she said to him, trying her damnedest to look seventeen as she stood in front of his desk.

He came around the desk and sat on the edge. "How'd you end up in Palm Cove?"

"My parents thought I'd have a better chance of getting into college if I graduated from an American high school."

"Your folks still over there?"

She nodded.

"What kind of work do they do?"

"They're missionaries," she said, and saw a brief look of surprise flick on and off his face. She tried to look properly pious or virginal or whatever the children of missionaries were supposed to look like. In actuality, she knew a lot of them were holy terrors.

He seemed to become a little more respectful at the word *missionary*. Like everyone else in the class, he had probably never met one.

"Sorry I gave you a hard time on your first day," he said, "but you were the only one in there who looked wide awake."

Jill almost told him it was okay, then changed her mind. She didn't want to give him license to do it again.

"Well, listen, it's nice to have someone different in class."

"Thanks," she said.

"Can I offer a little advice?"

"Sure."

"Sit up front, you'll get more out of class."

Good advice, except what she wanted to get out of class wasn't a knowledge of current events.

"Thanks."

"Go on," he said. "You're going to be late to your next class."

ENGLISH WAS OKAY. Jill didn't mind English. What she wasn't looking forward to was next period, which was lunch. Maybe she was only a fake student, but lunch hour was always crucial, and probably particularly so in a new school. She could remember high school perfectly clearly, and kids always sat with their own groups. On the rare occasions her high school got a new student, she could remember how the girls, being the snotty high school girls that they were, would always ignore the new girl until she proved herself. And one of the best ways of ignoring her was freezing her out at lunch if she had the audacity to sit at their table.

Of course she had an advantage in that she wasn't trying to be popular or get into a good group or even make friends. In fact she'd be a lot better off if she didn't. She had a feeling, though, that just having that kind of attitude could almost guarantee her popularity. It was probably unknown for a new student not to give a damn, and an attitude like that would be intriguing.

Jill had been given three choices of senior English: drama, journalism or poetry. She had chosen drama because it sounded easy, which was probably a mistake as the class was ninety percent girls and none of the boys even remotely resembled the "prince" her sister had fallen for.

The class was reading *Macbeth* out loud and it sounded just as boring to her now as it had sounded when she was a teenager. She was sitting in the back so she used the occasion to open her algebra book and take a look at tonight's homework.

It looked impossible. She didn't even have a clue what all that writing meant. She could as easily decipher cuneiform. And what was really dumb, really stupid, was that she didn't mind making an idiot of herself by sitting in the back with the jocks, but it really bothered her that she was going to flunk any test they might have in algebra. She wasn't used to looking like a dummy.

She was finally called on to hold forth as Lady Macbeth for a while, and she read it in the dull monotone that everyone else in the class seemed partial to. She looked up at one point and saw the teacher, a pretty woman in her early forties, grimace at the reading, and Jill wondered what kept her in a job that must be less than rewarding to someone with such an obvious love of Shakespeare. Anyone who longed to hear Shakespeare read well didn't belong in your average high school.

When the bell rang, Jill followed half the school down the hall to the cafeteria. The other half ate forty minutes later.

The cafeteria was bright and cheerful and air-conditioned, which was more than she could say for her alma mater. The trays were molded plastic rather than aluminum, the food even looked fairly healthy, but she avoided the salads like everyone else and picked up a hamburger, fries, chocolate milk and green Jell-o. After the endless meals of *we't* on *injera* in Ethiopia, she couldn't get enough of good old American junk food.

She casually surveyed the cafeteria after paying the cashier. She saw the jocks from civics at a table with several more jocks. She saw the three blond cheerleader types sitting with several more blond cheerleader types. She saw a table of serious-looking students, which she was really going to avoid since "serious" meant "intelligent" and "intelligent" meant she might not fool them as easily as the others. She saw an empty table, which probably wouldn't be empty long, but she gave it a try.

As she approached the table of jocks, one of them called out, "Hey, there's Africa!"

She knew they thought it would embarrass her, that she'd blush and be humiliated and might even drop her tray. Well, they had another think coming.

"Hi, guys," she said, flashing them a smile and winking at the blond who had sat next to her in civics. She might as well lower her standards and get a reputation as a flirt. In her experience, boys liked flirts, and getting the boys to like her was crucial to her success.

She saw the boy she had winked at rolling his eyes in embarrassment as the other boys started giving him a hard time about the "new girl." She passed by their table and took a seat at the empty table nearest the cafeteria door. She planned on eating fast and making an early escape.

A few minutes later the other end of the table had filled up but the spaces around her remained empty. She could tell she was getting some curious looks but ignored them.

She couldn't ignore the fat redheaded girl who sat down across from her. "Hi," the girl said.

Jill smiled at her. "Hi."

"Where're you from?"

"I've been living in Africa."

The girl's eyes widened. "No kidding?"

Jill nodded.

"I was wondering where you went to high school that they dressed like that. That's how my mom dresses."

"I dress like your *mother*?"

"That's all my mother ever wears, jeans and T-shirts. I think she used to be a hippie."

"I didn't know short skirts were in style," said Jill, and now that she did know she still wasn't going to wear them. If you weren't worried about being popular, you didn't have to worry about dressing like everyone else. Anyway, she couldn't afford a new wardrobe.

"Yeah, unfortunately," said the girl.

"Well, I never felt it was necessary to dress in style," said Jill. That was the truth now, but not when she'd been in high school.

"My name's Phaedra," the girl said, watching Jill closely for her reaction.

Jill thought the hippie mother ought to be boiled in oil for branding her daughter like that. "Well, Phaedra, you're pretty brave for sitting with me. I was beginning to feel like a leper."

"I could tell you were scared in algebra."

"Humiliated's more like it. Obviously what they thought they were teaching us as algebra in Africa bears no resemblance to the real thing. I don't know whether to drop it or just wait and flunk out."

"I'd offer to help you, but I'm not so good at algebra myself."

"I'll just have to burn a little midnight oil."

"What?"

"Stay up late," Jill translated for her.

"I wish I were like you," said Phaedra.

Thin? Blond? She didn't quite know how to answer.

"You have self-confidence," explained Phaedra. "You don't care what anyone thinks of you. I try to be like that, but it never works."

"I really don't care," said Jill. "There's no way a new student near the end of senior year is going to make friends and suddenly be popular. I just want to get my degree and get out of here."

"Yeah, me too."

The three blond cheerleader-types came by, paused for a moment by the table, then shook their heads and moved on.

"Who're the three bleached blondes?" Jill asked Phaedra. Phaedra choked on her food.

"Melanie, Marla and Mindy. We call them the M&Ms. They're the most popular girls in the school."

"I'll bet they're cheerleaders."

"Don't tell me you had blond cheerleaders in Africa."

"No," said Jill, "but I know the type. We had them in Michigan, too."

"You're from Michigan?" asked Phaedra.

"Originally," said Jill.

"I had a friend from Michigan," said Phaedra, "but she killed herself."

It took all of Jill's nerves, all her concentration, not to fall apart at the news that this girl had known Susan. She had been stupid to mention Michigan, but if she hadn't she might never have found this out.

Trying very hard to sound only mildly curious, she said, "Killed herself?"

Phaedra nodded. "She drowned herself."

"How awful."

Phaedra didn't say anything but she looked upset.

"Were you very good friends?"

"She was nice to me."

"Why did she do it?"

Phaedra shrugged as she filled her mouth with food.

"That must have been terrible for you."

Phaedra nodded and looked as though she were wishing she'd never mentioned it.

Jill decided it wasn't the time to question her any further. Phaedra looked shaken and it was more than likely that she had imagined a friendship when Susan had only been kind.

"Want to show me where the ladies' room is?" she asked her.

Phaedra started to giggle. "Ladies' room, that sounds so funny. It's just the girls' room."

That was the second time she had slipped up and she'd better watch it. If she slipped up at the wrong time and with the wrong people, she ran the risk of being thrown out of school before she found out anything. And she'd better stop coming across like an older sister to Phaedra and start acting the age she was supposed to be.

The girls' room smelled like a gas chamber from all the hair spray being whisked around. The M&Ms were in there applying makeup to their faces and mousse to their hair. Jill had no makeup and her hair looked best with her fingers pushed through it.

One of them looked at Jill's reflection in the mirror and asked, "Are you really from Africa?"

"I'm not *from* there," Jill said, "I was just living there."

"Why would you want to live there?"

"My parents are missionaries," she told her, knowing even as she said it what kind of reaction it would get.

She wasn't wrong. The blonde instantly dismissed her as being too boring for words.

Jill couldn't blame her. That would have been her reaction, too, before getting to know some of the missionaries in Africa. She wished she were a better kind of person, the kind who didn't care what others thought about them. She was a fake student and still it bothered her to have to pretend to what she wasn't.

"Don't let them bother you," Phaedra whispered to her on their way out of the washroom.

Jill shrugged, at the same time trying to pretend that she cared deep down.

"They don't like anyone," said Phaedra. "That's why they're popular."

Jill's true self popped out for a moment. "Maybe that works for them in high school," she told Phaedra, "but it sure isn't going to work for them in college."

"Wishful thinking," said Phaedra.

Jill was about to argue, then reined herself in. "You're right," she said, "it is wishful thinking."

And maybe thinking she was going to find something out by posing as a high school student was wishful thinking, too. But if she didn't do it, she'd never discover the truth about Susan's death. One thing was certain: she was convinced that Susan hadn't committed suicide.

"What do you have next?" Phaedra asked her.

"Spanish."

"Oh, too bad. I'm taking French. I really hate having to take a foreign language."

"Believe me, it comes in handy," Jill told her.

"Oh, yea, I forgot. What do they speak in Ethiopia?"

"In the cities you can get away with English, but where I was everyone mostly spoke Amharic."

"Let me hear you say something?"

"*Ameseghinalehu.*"

Phaedra looked impressed. "What does that mean?"

"Thank you."

"That sounds worse than French."

Just saying the word had suddenly made Jill feel homesick. Maybe she was being selfish trying to ease her parents' pain, when she could be back in Africa easing the pain of countless starving people.

But Susan was dead, and someone had to do something.

Chapter Two

Doug caught up with Trader outside the faculty dining room. "Let's get out of here. I'm buying," said Doug.

Trader stopped with his hand on the swinging door. "*You're* buying?"

"That's what I said."

"A rich relative die you didn't tell me about, Lacayo?"

"Come on, I need to get out of here."

"I know you didn't get a raise."

Doug grabbed his arm and started to hustle him down the hall. "I'm not in the mood for the company of teachers today," he said.

"I'm a teacher."

"P.E.? You consider that teaching, Woleski?"

"I'd say that it has a little more substance than civics. I mean, what do you have to do to teach civics—read the newspaper in the morning?"

"At least I read it."

"I don't have to read it," said Trader. "I know that if anything of monumental importance happens, I'll hear about it from you."

"Does the affluence around here ever get to you, Woleski?"

"What affluence? I'm always broke."

"At least you're not starving to death."

"I'm pretty hungry."

"I mean *starving*," said Doug.

"What's with you?" asked Trader.

"I don't know. I guess I'm feeling guilty."

"About what?"

"About the fact that I'm on my way to lunch and I can have anything I want to eat."

"Can I have anything I want?"

"I said I was buying; I didn't say I intended going bankrupt."

As Doug edged his Chevy out of the parking lot between the more expensive cars of the students, he said, "I'm not going to sign the contract."

"When did you decide that?"

"I can't do it. I can't take one more year of this."

"You said the same thing about Chicago."

"That was different. There's got to be a happy medium between inner-city schools where you worry every time a student puts his hand in his pocket, and this place where all the kids care about is growing up to make as much money as their fathers."

"You know what your problem is, Doug?"

"Burn-out."

"You're too idealistic, that's the problem."

"What's the matter with being idealistic?"

"It's not realistic, that's what," said Trader.

"Did anyone ever tell you you were a philosopher, Woleski?"

"No."

"Good, 'cause they'd be lying."

"I know what you need," said Trader.

"I'm glad you know, because I'll be damned if I do."

"We'll drive down to Miami tonight, pick up some women, and tomorrow you'll feel different."

"The old Woleski remedy, huh?"

"You got it."

"I don't feel like it," said Doug.

"You don't *feel* like it?"

"That's what I said."

"What is it, that time of month?"

"There's got to be more to life than picking up women in Miami."

"What?" asked Trader, looking genuinely bewildered.

"Don't you ever want to get serious about someone?"

"What for?"

"I don't understand you, Woleski."

"Have I changed? Wasn't I always like this?"

"Yeah, you were," Doug had to admit.

"So what's the problem?"

"The problem is, we're both going to be thirty soon and we're still picking up women in Miami."

"Is there some age limit on this?"

"Wouldn't you like to meet some woman you could talk to?"

"About what?"

"Anything. The economy, the ozone layer, how you felt about Santa Claus when you were a kid."

"Why would I want to talk about that?"

"There's more to life than sports, Woleski."

"Name one thing."

"I'm just saying it'd be nice to have a woman to talk to."

"I talk to them. What do you think, I don't talk to them? I give 'em compliments, make a little small talk. I know what they want to hear."

"Forget it. Where do you want to eat?"

"The problem with you, Doug, is you think they're like us. They're not. It's like they're a different species. You think you'd like to be buddies with them, but it ain't gonna happen."

"McDonald's or Burger King?"

"You're buying—you decide."

The town was so affluent they didn't even allow fast-food restaurants, which meant he had to spend gas money to get out of town in order to eat somewhere he could afford.

Palm Cove made him feel like a second-class citizen.

TRADER CAME BACK from the counter with two more orders of fries and handed one to Doug. "I tell the team not to eat this junk."

"They eat it anyway," said Doug.

"Everyone eats it."

"I had a new girl in class today."

"And?"

"I don't know, she's different."

"You going for high school girls these days, Lacayo?"

"I don't *go* for her. She's just kind of different for this school, that's all."

"You mean she's not a blonde?"

"No, she's blond."

"Then what's so different about her?"

"She transferred here from Ethiopia."

"Where's that, northern Florida?"

"Even a jock like you isn't that stupid, Woleski."

"You mean the kid's actually from Africa?"

Doug nodded. "Her parents are missionaries."

"She must be weird, huh?"

"I don't know. Maybe. There was something about her, though. She had this awareness in her eyes that you never see in those kids. She looked like she knew something no one else did."

"Hell, anyone who's lived in Ethiopia would have to look aware. I'm surprised she doesn't look shell-shocked."

"Yeah, I guess."

"She good-looking?"

"She's not your type."

"I know she's not my type," said Trader. "High school girls aren't my type."

"She looks okay. Not flashy like most of them."

"Some of those girls ought to be locked up until they're legal," said Trader.

"She sat in the back row with the jocks."

"That takes guts."

"It didn't even seem to bother her."

"What does she know, she's been living in Africa."

"Yeah, I guess."

"I can't believe you're going to give all this up, Lacayo. Here I rescue you from Chicago, where even as we speak they're probably being buried in a couple of feet of spring snow, and you're going to give it all up."

"A year's enough. It's like one long vacation here. Summer vacation."

"You're complaining about that?"

"Even good weather can get monotonous."

"That's no reason to quit," said Trader.

"Look, if I thought I was making any difference..."

"Were you making any in Chi?"

"I think I'm going to get out of teaching alto-gether."

"And do what?"

"I don't know. That's the problem."

"Take the baseball team to the playoffs, and one of the proud fathers will probably offer you a job selling yachts."

"Those jobs go to over-the-hill pros. Anyway, I don't feel like selling yachts."

"So what do you feel like doing?"

"Maybe I'll go back for my doctorate."

"And do what, teach college?"

"It's got to be better than this."

"Look at it this way, Lacayo, some of the kids you're teaching this year will be in college next year. You really think they're going to go through some big change over the summer and start getting excited about current events? No way, they'll be exactly the same."

"I'm having a mid-life crisis and you're not being any help."

"Twenty-nine is not exactly mid-life."

"It feels like it."

Trader put his arm around Doug's shoulder and squeezed. "I tell you what, buddy. We'll forget about picking up women tonight and instead go out and tie one one. I think you've got spring fever."

"How can you tell in south Florida?"

JILL TRIED NOT TO SMILE with satisfaction all during Spanish class. After college she had been with the Peace Corps in Central America for two years before signing on with the World Health Services in Africa, and her Spanish was fluent, albeit colloquial.

It was beginning to look as though the only class she was going to have to concentrate on was algebra, and the rest of the time she could get down to some serious detective work. In fact the only thing she was going to have to worry about in Spanish was not sounding as accomplished as she was.

She couldn't wait to get out Susan's letters that night and start going over them for clues. She had written often and in volume, the letters of the past few months making frequent references to "the prince" she had fallen for. Tonight Jill would make a list of all the references and compare them with the boys she had met so far. One of them had to be the prince, and the prince had to know more about Susan's alleged suicide than he was saying. Not that he had said anything officially, or even come forward. If he had cared at all about Susan, though, he must be feeling guilty.

And, while she was at it, she'd see if her sister had ever mentioned her civics teacher. Just for investigative purposes, of course.

Jill was still thinking about Mr. Lacayo when she walked into seventh period study hall and saw that he was in charge. She took a seat at the back of the class and took out her algebra book. The class was two-thirds of the way through the text, but maybe if she started at the beginning it would make some sense to her.

A good-looking, dark-haired boy slid into the desk next to hers and took out the same book, opening it to the page of Jill's homework assignment. He saw her looking over at him and gave her a smile.

Jill smiled back before turning to the beginning of the book. The beginning didn't make any more sense to her It was an Algebra I book she needed, not Algebra II.

She glanced over at the boy next to her and watched as he quickly solved the problems. She looked up and saw Mr. Lacayo's eyes on her and quickly looked back down at her own book. She didn't know why she cared what he thought of her, but she didn't want him to think she was copying someone else's homework. It was probably ego, pure and simple. She had never needed to copy anyone's work in school and had always prided herself on her good mind. She thought maybe everyone with an ego like that might benefit from going back to high school for a day in order to see how well they survived.

"You need any help?" she heard in a whisper, and looked up to see the boy next to her speaking.

"I need more than help—I need a miracle."

"You in Colwin's class?"

She nodded.

"You can copy my homework, if you want."

"That doesn't solve the problem," said Jill.

"Didn't they teach you algebra in Africa?"

"Does the whole school know I'm from Africa already?"

He grinned. "I'm in your civics class."

She looked him over more carefully this time since he could conceivably be the prince. He looked like a prince, but then so did half the male students. Was it the ocean air and the Florida sun that made them so good-looking? She couldn't remember half a dozen boys in her high school who had looked so good.

She glanced to the front of the room and saw that Lacayo was watching them. She didn't think it was because they were whispering, because whispering was going on all over the room. Was he suspicious of her already? Was her age showing?

"I'm Alan," the boy was saying to her, giving her now what was sure to be his idea of a sexy smile. Well, it *was* sexy. It was just that he was too young.

"Jill," she said.

"I know."

He was looking at her in a way she used to wish a couple of the boys in her high school would look at her. Maybe she had found the perfect guy who thought that jeans were sexier than miniskirts and boyish haircuts more appealing than masses of platinum-blond hair, but she doubted it. Guys—even guys his age—didn't think like that.

He was still watching her, so she pointed to one of the equations at the beginning of the book and said, "Could you explain that to me in simple terms?"

"You've come to the right person. I'm a mathematical genius."

He slid his desk over so that it was up against hers, and then, in a low voice and with some expert pencil work on his paper, he did indeed explain it. "Now you try it," he told her, turning over the sheet of paper so that she couldn't see how he had done it.

She worked it out for herself. Maybe not with his speed, but she got it right.

"Good, now try the next two," he said.

She had trouble on the second one, but as soon as he started to point out her error, she found she understood what she was doing. It was a start, but she still had most of the book to do before she got caught up with the class.

"Thanks," she told him.

"Anytime."

"Do you need help with anything?"

"You mean schoolwork?"

She nodded.

"Not really."

She looked up again to see if Lacayo was still watching her. He wasn't, but half the girls in the class were. And they all looked jealous. She felt like announcing to the group at large, "Don't worry about me, I'm not after this kid," but she had a feeling none of them would believe her.

She was well into the chapter when the bell rang. Her final class of the day was P.E. and she wasn't looking forward to it. She had looked her body over very carefully in the shower that morning, searching for any signs of aging, and while she seemed to measure up in her own eyes, she was pretty sure that teenage girls were going to be more critical. She didn't sag nor have cellulite, but her body had to show some signs of wear and tear over the past ten years. If nothing else, it was going to look pretty strange when they saw her suntan ended where her short sleeves began.

It wasn't her uneven tan that was commented on in the girls' locker room, however; it was her white cotton underpants. And she should have known better, too. She had also worn minute bikini underwear in high school, and even in college. But what you needed in Africa to keep from getting diaper rash was good old-fashioned cotton.

As she changed into the navy shorts and white shirt worn for P.E., she could hear the voice of one of the M&Ms remarking on her panties, and she wasn't trying not to be overheard.

"My baby sister used to wear those," the girl was saying. "I think you call them training pants." Her disciples dutifully giggled and looked over at Jill.

Since P.E. was going to be tennis today, Jill looked over at the cheerleader and said, "Yes, and what I'm in training for is tennis." She was throwing out a challenge and saw that the girl understood.

"I didn't know they played tennis in Africa," said the cheerleader.

"The conditions are primitive, of course, but we managed to hit the ball around."

"Challenge her to a game, Marla," said one of the girls, egging her on.

"Two out of three?" asked Marla.

Okay, so she hadn't played tennis in Africa. She had played on the women's team in college and it was like bicycle riding, you never forgot. "I'd be delighted," said Jill.

Marla turned out to have a backhand like Martina Navratilova, and playing tennis turned out to be not at all like riding a bicycle.

JILL TURNED ON the air conditioner when she got home and got a pint of strawberry ice cream out of the refrigerator. The garage apartment was small, but it seemed luxurious to her with air-conditioning, screens on the windows, cool tile floors, a soft bed and hot water whenever she wanted it. There was even a small color TV and over the weekend she had watched it almost non-stop. It had more channels than she had ever seen, and some of the channels had programs she didn't think were allowed on television. The Wyckoffs had a swimming pool in the backyard they had told her she was welcome to use, but tempting as it sounded, she couldn't wait to get out her sister's letters and start going over them for clues.

She carried the ice cream over to the desk, picked up the phone and punched out a local number. Another luxury—she hadn't seen a push-button phone in years.

"How did it go?" her mother asked her, sounding sad and strained and unsure of herself and not at all the way Jill remembered her sounding. Back when Jill was in high school, her mother had sounded like the professional she was, and most of the time Jill had found her intimidating. Now she just felt sorry for her.

"It was terrifying," Jill told her. "I couldn't remember one thing in algebra."

"But you were always so good in school."

"Well, now I know what it feels like not to be smart."

"I really don't know why you're doing this, dear."

"I don't know, Mom. I guess I felt I had to do something."

"The police already—"

"The police didn't do anything," said Jill, "except call it a suicide. Unless there's something you're not telling me, my little sister was not suicidal. She wrote me letters all the time, Mom, and mostly they were funny. Come on, how much of a sense of humor do you have if you're contemplating suicide?"

"If only we hadn't moved here—"

"Just stop it with the guilt. Okay, so she didn't want to move here, but once she got here she loved it. If you don't believe me, I'll show you her letters."

"She seemed to like it, but your sister wasn't much of a complainer. You were different. I always knew what was on your mind because you always spoke it."

"Well, I'm still speaking it, and I'm telling you to quit feeling guilty because it wasn't your fault. I still think it was an accident and I'm going to do my best to prove it."

"I went in your sister's room today, thinking I ought to go through her things."

Jill felt her throat tighten up. "There's no rush, Mom."

"I know."

"That reminds me, I was dressed all wrong for school. Why didn't you tell me they didn't wear jeans anymore?"

"I think you could fit into your sister's clothes."

"Someone might recognize them."

"Well, I know how you girls don't like to look different."

"That was high school, Mom. I don't mind looking different anymore."

"Did you fool everyone?"

"I think so. But then kids don't have any conception of age."

"You still look like a girl to me. But that isn't what I wanted to say. I found a diary hidden in Susan's underwear drawer."

"Did it say anything?"

"I didn't feel I had a right to read it."

"Oh, Mom, it's too late for that. And maybe it would tell us something."

"I think that's what I was afraid of. If she's written any thoughts about suicide, I don't think I could stand to read them."

"I want to read it, Mom."

"I thought you would."

"I can't come by for it, someone might see me and wonder."

"I've called Carol Wyckoff and they're going out to dinner with us tonight. I'll give it to her for you. Incidentally, Carol says she hasn't seen anything of you since you moved in."

"I don't want to be a bother."

"They're old friends. They wouldn't mind."

"Look, they're doing enough letting me use this apartment."

"How is it?"

"The height of luxury."

"I really doubt that. It's where the gardener used to live."

"Believe me, compared to where I live in Ethiopia, it's a palace."

"It's probably just as well I've never visited you there."

"Mom, are you okay?"

"No, I'm not okay. But I'm very glad to have you nearby. We missed you, you know."

"I know, Mom."

"Not that we aren't very proud of the work you're doing."

"I know." She could feel tears threatening and knew her mother must be feeling the same way. In an effort to cheer her up, she said, "Guess what, Mom?"

"What?"

"I have a crush on one of my teachers."

"Oh, dear."

"Mom, it's okay, he couldn't be more than a year or two older than me."

"Yes, but *he* doesn't know that."

"He doesn't know I have a crush on him, either."

"Well, I guess that's better than dating high school boys at your age."

"Considerably better, and it makes the class go more quickly, too. The whole point of crushes in school is to alleviate the boredom."

"Jill, honey, be careful."

"Of what?"

"I don't know. I just don't want anything to happen to you, too."

"Don't worry, Mom, nothing's going to happen to me."

DOUG FELT ON EDGE and the beer wasn't doing anything to relax him. They had driven down to a beachfront bar in Lauderdale, and Trader was amusing himself by flirting with one of the barmaids, but Doug hadn't wanted to go out in the first place, and now that they were out he couldn't wait to go home.

He used to like going out. Lately, though, the feeling had come to him that it would be nice to stay home at night if he had someone nice to stay home with. And he didn't mean Trader. When Trader was home, sports were on the TV, and Doug had watched enough sports to last him the rest of his life. It would be nice to have someone at home to talk to. Someone to love. Ideally, a woman, but at the rate he was going he was never going to meet the right woman, so maybe he should settle for a dog.

"You like dogs?" he asked Trader.

Trader dragged his eyes away from the dark-haired barmaid. "What?"

"Dogs. I was thinking we should get a dog."

"Forget it," said Trader.

"I'll take care of it. You won't even know it's there."

"No dogs, Lacayo. Our lease says no pets of any kind." Trader turned back to the barmaid.

Doug couldn't get the picture out of his mind of Alan Singer and that new girl in study hall today. Alan was one of the savviest seniors in the school and he couldn't quite picture him being interested in the daughter of missionaries. He didn't trust that interest for a minute.

"What's your opinion of Singer?" Doug asked Trader.

Trader listened to the music for a minute. "I don't even know who's singing."

"*Alan* Singer."

"Smartest quarterback I've ever coached."

"He's bright, all right. I'll concede him that."

"A bit of a prima donna, but what the hell; all quarterbacks are."

"Yeah, but do you trust him?"

"Is he giving you a hard time on the team?"

"No, he's a great pitcher. Remarkable control."

"Then what's your problem, Lacayo?"

"Would you trust him with your sister?"

"Judy? She's thirty-five. Of course I'd trust him with Judy."

"You know what I mean, Woleski."

"I'm afraid I don't."

"Would you trust him with a nice, innocent high school girl?"

"You mean there is such a thing?"

"I'm serious."

"I can see you are, but this isn't anyplace to be serious in. In case you hadn't noticed, we're out partying."

"There's something about him I don't like."

"You want to know what it is?"

"That's what I'm trying to figure out."

"For starters, he's smarter than you. He tested out at something like genius. He's also better looking. He's also richer. He drives a new Porsche. The girls think he's the sexiest guy in the school. Shall I go on?"

"You really know how to make a guy feel good."

"You want to feel good? Drink your beer."

JILL SCANNED THE DIARY quickly the first time for any mention of Mr. Lacayo. There was none. She couldn't believe that her sister had sat in that man's class for several months and never even mentioned him by name. Was it possible that high school girls no longer noticed young, good-looking teachers? Had Susan been blind? If so, Susan had sure been different from her at that age.

Jill couldn't remember one school year, high school or college, when she hadn't had a crush on one teacher or another. The beauty of it was, it was safe, rather like having a crush on a rock star or Joe Montana.

It had been late when Mrs. Wyckoff had dropped off the diary, and Jill was having trouble keeping her eyes open. There was one thing she had to do, though, before turning in for the night. She read the last few entries in the diary for any signs of suicidal thoughts. She couldn't find any. And judging by the way her sister poured out her heart, if she had been thinking along those lines, Jill was sure Susan would have made mention of it in the diary. Anyway, that's what diaries were for—secret thoughts.

She called her mother, saying, "Did I wake you up?"

"No, honey, I'm not sleeping very well lately."

"Don't you have any sleeping pills?"

"If I refused to prescribe them for patients, I'm certainly not going to take them myself."

"Oh, Mom, one's not going to kill you."

"They're addictive, Jill."

"Well, maybe this will make you sleep better—there was nothing suicidal in the diary."

"I'm not sure you'd tell me if there was."

"Maybe not, but I'd probably not say *any*thing. Listen, Susan sounded happy and in love."

"In love? She wasn't even dating."

"Are you sure?"

"No boy ever came to the house to pick her up."

"Well, maybe it wasn't reciprocated, but she was in love. And if I can find out who he is, maybe I can find out what happened to her."

"She doesn't mention his name?"

"No. She calls him the prince."

"Darling, this is beginning to sound dangerous."

"Dangerous?"

"Boys have been known to kill their girlfriends out of jealousy. There was that case in New York just last year."

"Why would he be jealous? She was in love with him."

"It could've been another reason."

"Mom, are you sure she wasn't seeing anyone?"

"I would've known, Jill. It's not like when you were in high school and I was working all the time."

"No boys ever called her?"

"Oh, I think she got phone calls, but she didn't go out on dates."

"You mean she stayed home every weekend?"

"No, she went places. Parties and movies and things like that. She always said she was meeting friends."

"Yes, well I used to say that, too, if I didn't think you'd approve of the boy."

"Don't be ridiculous. Why wouldn't we approve of him?"

"I don't know."

"You're saying he was someone dangerous?"

"I don't think it's anything like that, Mom. I think it's more likely it was an accident, and if any kids were around at the time, they were probably afraid to come forward. Kids panic and they don't like to tell on each other."

"You be careful."

"Hey, if I can take care of myself in Africa, I'm sure I can take care of myself in Palm Cove High School. Anyway, I just wanted to let you know it wasn't suicide. If she didn't sound unhappy in her letters to me, and she didn't mention it in her diary, and she seemed happy at home—hell, there has to be another explanation."

Her mother hadn't sounded any better when she hung up, but Jill wasn't going to give up hope. She knew that as long as her parents thought their younger daughter had killed herself, they were going to torture themselves with guilt. If Jill could prove it was an accident, they still might never get over the loss; in fact she was sure they wouldn't, but at least they wouldn't endlessly blame themselves. And maybe Jill would stop blaming herself for not being around when Susan had needed her.

She put the diary in the drawer of the bedside table and decided she'd start on it after school tomorrow and write down all the references to the prince. Right after she finished her homework, that is.

She turned off the light and slid down in the bed. She had the air conditioner on high and it was lovely to be able to sleep under a comforter when the temperature outside was near eighty and not have to contend with mosquito netting.

She went over her first day of school in her mind and wasn't satisfied with the picture. She had felt incredibly stupid in algebra; the only girl who seemed to like her was a girl not liked by anyone else; a good-looking boy was coming on to her in study hall, but he probably thought she looked easy; she had been royally shown up in P.E. by a cheerleader type; and she was developing a crush on a man who thought she was seventeen.

Not exactly an auspicious start.

Chapter Three

Today I met my prince. I walked into civics class and there he was. I was dressed all wrong and feeling out of place and wishing we had never moved to Florida. Then I saw him and I knew the move was fate. I've fallen in love before, but never like this. Never this suddenly. I don't think he even noticed me. After school I got Mom to take me shopping.

JILL SAT IN HOME ROOM and ignored the announcements as she silently berated her investigative abilities. It was Friday already and she wasn't any closer to finding out what happened to Susan than she had been when she started school on Monday.

A group of jocks acted friendly to her but it would be a miracle if the prince turned out to be one of them. She had antagonized the popular girls and for all she knew they might have been friendly with Susan and able to tell her something. She had Phaedra following her around like a long-lost friend, but Phaedra wasn't forthcoming whenever she brought up Susan's name. She hadn't even finished perusing Susan's diary because her homework, and algebra, was taking up all her time. And she had a crush on a teacher who would probably think she was some kind of nymphet if he knew about it.

At least the weekend was coming up. She sure could use it. Unlike real high school, when weekends had meant dates and parties and movies and shopping at the mall, she would have nothing to do but hole up in her apartment and try to figure out where she was going from here. It was beginning to look as if all she was getting out of the mission was refresher courses in high school subjects.

And what really annoyed her was the fact that she *didn't* have a date for Saturday night. She was reliving all the drudge work of high school without any of the perks.

Susan, she reminded herself. *You're here to find out what happened to Susan.* But, sadly enough, she couldn't even picture Susan in her mind. She tried, but all she could come up with was Susan's junior high graduation picture her parents had sitting on their piano in a silver frame alongside her own high school graduation picture. That picture brought back the days when she thought hair was something to fuss over and clothes were something to covet.

Things didn't brighten up when she walked into Mr. Colwin's algebra class and saw him putting a test on the board. She took a seat, took out a piece of paper and wrote her name at the top. After that it was all downhill. She had worked her way almost halfway through the book, but she didn't have a clue how to solve the problems on the test.

Very slowly, and very slyly, she found herself doing something she had never done in her life. She started copying from the girl seated next to her. She told herself it didn't actually count since she wasn't really a student and wouldn't receive a grade for the course, but she still felt guilty.

What she had never realized before was how easy it was. She didn't have to turn her head or even raise it. All she had to do was shift her eyes to the right and pretend to be doing the work herself. The girl didn't even look up and catch her at it. At the end of the class when she passed her test in with the rest, she could feel herself blushing. She felt like the worst kind of criminal and yearned to confess. It would serve her right if the paper she copied had all wrong answers.

She was still feeling guilty when she walked into civics and took her seat in the back row. David, the blond who sat next to her, smiled at her and said hi, and she could smell liquor on his breath. Ten twenty-five in the morning and he'd been drinking? Actually she could use a drink herself. Alan, who sat on the other side of David, leaned forward and asked, "How's the algebra coming?" Before she could answer, Mr. Lacayo walked into the class and the students quieted down.

Jill opened her notebook, wrote, "We had a test," then pulled out the paper and handed it over to Alan.

When the paper was passed back to her, he had written, "How did you do?"

She wrote back, "I faked it," and held up the paper for him to read. What she didn't want was to be caught writing notes in Lacayo's class. He thought she was juvenile enough without reverting to that. And yet the funny thing was, being back in school made her feel juvenile again. She felt like writing notes. She watched the minutes tick off the clock. She longed to ditch school and go to the beach. She had to suppress an urge to write Mr. Lacayo's name on the cover of her notebook. In short, she was beginning to feel seventeen again.

Lacayo was asking the class what the major news story had been in the morning's paper and no one was saying a word.

"Hey, you guys awake?" he asked the class.

"Barely," murmured someone near the front.

Mr. Lacayo walked around to the front of his desk and sat on the edge. His hair looked slightly damp as though he'd just taken a shower. Not that Mr. Lacayo taking a shower was something she ought to be thinking about, but damn it, she was human, wasn't she?

Lacayo caught her staring at him and said, "How about you, Jill, did you read the paper this morning?"

"I was still doing my homework this morning," said Jill, loving the freedom to be able to say things she never dared say in high school.

He shook his head and put on his beleaguered look. Jill loved that look. "Doesn't anyone listen to the radio?" he asked.

Several kids nodded.

"So what did you hear?" he asked, getting the names of songs shouted out to him in reply.

"Don't you care what's going on in the world?"

Jill could tell him what was going on in the world. People in Ethiopia were going barefoot while the students here seemed to have a different pair of shoes for every day of the week. Enough food was thrown away in the cafeteria in one day to keep a hundred starving people alive for a week. And Susan's death was being called a suicide.

"Does the word AK-47 ring a bell?" asked Lacayo.

"That's an assault rifle," said one of the boys.

Lacayo nodded. "And yesterday it was used to kill seven people at a shopping mall in Miami."

The boys seemed to perk up at the news, but one of the girls said in a bored tone, "People are always getting killed in Miami."

"The gun laws in Miami are some of the most relaxed in the country," said Lacayo, "but whenever anyone tries to do something about it, the NRA says, 'Guns don't kill people, people kill people.'"

He allowed that to sink in for a moment, although as far as Jill could tell, no one was paying much attention.

"How many of you have guns in your houses?" he asked, and Jill was shocked to see every hand but hers go up.

Feeling bored and a little argumentative, she raised her hand.

"Yes, Jill?"

"It *is* people who do the killing," she said.

"You can kill seven people with an assault rifle a lot faster and with a lot more ease than if you had to run around strangling them," said Lacayo.

She shook her head. "It's not the guns. There's something wrong with the people."

"Keep going," said Lacayo.

Jill, who had practically overdosed on newspapers since being back in the country, spoke her mind. "Parents are killing each other and their children. Children are killing their parents. Some people are killing strangers for the fun of it. Something is very wrong. In the African villages, every man has a spear, but he doesn't kill his family with it."

"Will you admit that a lack of gun control isn't helping?" He was talking to her now as though they were the only two in the room, and what had started off as a mild flirtation on her part was becoming serious.

"Those homeless men who are being killed in Palm Cove aren't being killed with guns. People are killing each other for sport."

Lacayo seemed to be enjoying it. "Will you at least concede that there would be less killing if there were fewer guns?"

"If someone wants to kill, he'll find a way," said Jill.

"He?" asked Lacayo, pouncing on the pronoun.

"It's usually a he," said Jill. "Men seem to have a thing about guns that most women don't seem to have."

"My mom has a gun," one of the girls spoke up, and then several more of the students said the same thing.

"Okay," said Jill, "maybe I'm wrong, but all of the killings with guns I've read about in the newspaper since I've been here have been done by men."

Lacayo grinned at her. "Much as I hate to admit you're right, you're right. It usually is a male." He looked around the classroom as though wanting to draw some of the others into the discussion. "Do you all agree with Jill?" he asked. "Do you all think it's okay for everyone to carry guns?"

"I didn't say that," said Jill.

"That's what it sounded like."

"I'm just saying it isn't the fault of the guns. There could be a hundred thousand guns sitting in a pile in front of the school, and they wouldn't be a danger to anyone until the first person picked one up."

"Then you think we need gun control to protect ourselves from ourselves?"

"I think we have to learn to respect life, that's all," said Jill. "And that includes animals as well."

"Spoken like a true missionary's daughter," said Alan, and there was some general laughter, mostly of relief. The subject seemed a little heavy for the class.

There was quiet for a moment, then, "Well, on a lighter note, does anyone know what bill the president vetoed yesterday?"

"I HEAR YOU GOT in an argument with Lacayo this morning," Phaedra said to her at lunch.

"How'd you hear that?"

"News gets around."

"That's news?"

"You might not realize it, Jill, but the school's buzzing about you. You're a big topic of conversation around here."

"Why me?"

"You dress different, you talk different, your parents are missionaries. But mostly I think it's because Alan Singer's taken an interest in you."

"You mean the Alan who's helping me with algebra?"

Phaedra nodded.

"What is it—is this the first time anyone's ever helped anyone else around here?"

"It's just that half the girls in the school are after him and he seems interested in you."

"He's not interested in me. He just helps me out in study hall, that's all."

"Alan is not exactly known as a good Samaritan."

"Well, I'm not interested in him. I have a boyfriend in Africa."

"No kidding? What's his name?"

"Jack," she said, thinking of Jack Hansen, who was married to her best friend.

"Jack and Jill, that's cute," said Phaedra.

Jill laughed. "You're right, it's much too cutesy."

"I didn't mean that," said Phaedra.

"What does Lacayo do besides teach civics?" asked Jill.

"He also teaches U.S. history and coaches the baseball team."

"I haven't seen a baseball game in years."

"There's a game tonight. We're playing Boca Raton."

"Do many kids go to the games?"

"Not really. Not like football and basketball, but we've got a good team this year."

"Are you going?"

Phaedra shook her head.

"You want to go?"

"You mean with you?"

Jill nodded.

Phaedra's smile occupied half her face. "Yeah, I'd love to."

"Okay. I'll pick you up."

"Are you going because you want to see Alan play?"

"I didn't even know he was on the team."

"Sure, he's our star pitcher."

"No, I'm not going to see Alan play."

Phaedra looked as if she wanted to dispute that but was afraid Jill might change her mind about going. Oh, well, let her think it. It was better than having her think she wanted to go to see a teacher.

JILL PULLED UP to the address Phaedra had given her and parked the car. She didn't know whether to honk the horn or go to the door. She decided honking the horn was rude, even though that's all she had ever done when she was in high school.

Phaedra's mother answered the door and Jill was instantly on guard. As Phaedra had said, her mother dressed just like Jill in jeans, T-shirt and sneakers. She also looked a lot closer to Jill's age than Phaedra's.

"Is Phaedra home?" she asked, lowering her head to avoid the woman's scrutiny.

"Be right there, Jill," yelled Phaedra from somewhere in the house.

"You're the girl from Africa?" asked her mother.

Jill nodded, and the woman stepped back so that Jill could enter the house. The entry hall alone had enough house plants to remind her of the jungles of Central America.

"What's it like over there?" asked Phaedra's mother.

"Very poor," said Jill, "and very dry. Nothing's growing and everyone's starving."

"What do your parents do?"

Jill was certain Phaedra had told her mother. "They run a school over there and also a small clinic."

"I should be doing something like that," said Phaedra's mother. "I used to be so involved. Then we moved down here and now all I do is go to the beach and the malls."

Jill smiled at her, thinking it was ironic that she'd rather get to know Phaedra's mother than Phaedra.

Phaedra appeared, this time dressed in long pants rather than her usual miniskirt. It wasn't much of an improvement. The girl seemed overly excited about going somewhere with Jill, and Jill had the feeling she wasn't doing her any favor. What it came right down to it, she was using her.

IT WASN'T UNTIL the eighth inning that Jill realized Alan was pitching a no-hitter. There was a buzz in the stands and she overheard a man behind her say, "Four more outs and the kid's got it." Jill looked over at the scoreboard and saw the zeroes strung across the board.

"A no-hitter, this is exciting," said Jill.

"It'll be his third this season," said Phaedra. "I hear major league scouts are coming to see him."

Jill watched as Alan threw his third strike to the batter and the small crowd went wild. One more inning and he had it, and he didn't even look nervous. Jill was covered with sweat and Alan's shirt didn't even look damp. She wondered if his mathematical ability helped him with pitching.

Alan stood in front of the bench for a moment and seemed to be looking over the stands. When his eyes came to Jill, he nodded his head and she grinned at him.

"He's looking at you," said Phaedra, her voice full of wonder.

"We're kind of getting to be friends," said Jill.

"Friends? You want to be *friends* with him?"

"I told you I have a boyfriend."

"Yeah, but he's a long way away. And my mother says you're supposed to have lots of boyfriends in high school."

Jill looked over to where Lacayo stood. He appeared to be a low-key coach, never getting into disputes with the umpires, never yelling at his players. In fact he looked downright bored. She was rather bored, too. High school baseball wasn't her idea of excitement, and she began to wonder if it had been worth the waste of an evening just to see Lacayo standing around looking bored. She guessed it was. At least it beat staying home and watching television and wondering what he was doing.

David, who sat next to her in civics, was up to bat, and she found herself yelling out, "Let's go, David, let's get a hit." Several people turned around to look at her, including a few of the players on the bench.

"We don't need a hit," said Phaedra. "There's no way they can beat us at this point."

"I just felt like yelling."

Phaedra gave her a sly look. "Is it David you're interested in?"

"No, Phaedra."

"I hear he's not very bright."

"He's cute, though."

"Yeah, he's cute. If you like blondes."

"I have nothing against blondes," said Jill.

"I hear he drinks too much."

"He even drinks in school."

Phaedra looked at her. "Yeah? How do you know that?"

"I can smell it on his breath."

"Well, I guess it's better than taking drugs."

David hit a fly to left field that was easily caught and then Alan was up to bat. He got a big round of applause and then quickly struck out.

The tension was high when Boca Raton got up to bat in the ninth. The few fans that had followed them to the game seemed to have lost interest. They didn't boo their team, but they cheered each strike Alan sent across the plate. In less than five minutes the game was over and his teammates were crowding around him.

"You interested in him now?" asked Phaedra.

"Just because he got a no-hitter?"

Phaedra shrugged. "I'm beginning to think you don't like boys."

"They seem a little young, that's all."

"How old's your boyfriend?"

"Twenty."

"Oh." Phaedra sounded impressed.

"What about you?" Jill asked her. "You interested in anybody?"

"I have a huge crush on George Michael."

"Is he on the team?"

Phaedra looked at her in astonishment. "He's a rock star."

"I'm a little out of touch," said Jill.

"I guess."

They were headed out of the stands when she saw Alan approaching her, David and another boy right behind him.

"Great game," she said to him.

Alan grinned. "Did you come out to see me pitch?"

"It's the least I could do after all your help in algebra."

He started to say something to her, then looked over at Phaedra and closed his mouth as a look of distaste came over his face. Jill knew if you hung around with girls like Phaedra the boys didn't ask you anywhere, but that was just the kind of protection she wanted. Dating high school boys wasn't on her agenda.

"Well, see you around," said Alan, and he took off with his friends.

"I think he was going to ask you to go somewhere with him," said Phaedra.

"I doubt it," said Jill.

"I bet he would've if I hadn't been here."

"Then I'm glad you are," said Jill.

She knew she ought to ask Phaedra if there was some hangout she wanted to stop at before going home, but she didn't think she could stand any more teenage life for the night. Sitting around over Cokes and French fries while talking about boys didn't sound like much fun to her.

Now if Lacayo were going to be there, that would be different. She saw him across the field talking to Boca Raton's coach. He seemed to be looking at her, but he was probably only looking at the people filing out of the stands. She wondered where he was going now. For all she knew he had a steady woman. Or even a wife.

That thought was enough to depress her.

SHE WAS HALFWAY HOME after dropping off Phaedra when she realized she was being followed. The other car wasn't being sneaky about it; it was right on her tail, its headlights lighting up her car like daylight.

When she pulled up in front of the Wyckoff's house, the car pulled in right behind her and cut its lights. She got out of the car, locked up and looked over at the other car.

Alan stuck his head out of the window. "Is this where you live?"

She walked back to his car. "No, I always park in strange neighborhoods." She saw that David was in the passenger seat and one of the other jocks was in the back seat.

"You know Mark?" Alan asked her, motioning with his head towards the dark-haired boy in the back.

"Hi, Mark," said Jill.

"I'm in civics with you," said Mark.

"Everyone's in civics with me." Maybe Mark was the prince and she ought to pay more attention.

"Nice house," said Alan, looking over the fourteen-room fake Moorish castle.

"It belongs to my aunt and uncle," said Jill.

"I guess missionaries don't live like that."

"Not in Africa, anyway," said Jill.

"So you enjoy living in luxury?"

"Actually I live over the garage."

"Right."

"I mean it. I have my own apartment."

"I don't believe you," said Alan. "No high school kid is that lucky."

"Come on up and I'll show you," said Jill.

Alan looked a little taken aback by that, as though it was the kind of thing he might say to a girl, but never expected a girl to say to him.

"Maybe she wants to show you her etchings," joked Mark.

"No etchings," said Jill, "and I meant all of you."

"You got any beer up there?" asked Alan.

"Sorry," said Jill, shaking her head.

Mark lifted up a six pack from the back seat. "Mind if we bring this?"

"Not at all, I'd love a beer," she said, then wondered if inviting high school boys into her apartment for beer was something that could get her arrested. Probably, but this was too good a chance to miss. If one of them was the prince, maybe he would slip up.

Alan looked doubtful up to the moment where she actually opened the door to the apartment with her own key and let them inside. She turned on the overhead light and the kitchen light.

"Not bad," said Alan, looking around.

"Not a Moorish castle, but it's all mine."

"I can't believe they let you live here alone," said Mark, handing her a can of beer.

"Why not? I'm responsible. It's not like I have boys up here or anything." That got a laugh out of them.

"Got a stereo?" asked David.

"No, that's the only thing I don't have. If you want some music, put on MTV."

"So tell me something," said Alan, sinking down into the overstuffed couch. "Why do you hang around with Phaedra? You're going to scare off the boys that way."

"If that's true what are the three of you doing here?"

Alan smiled in enjoyment. "You're different, you know it? Any other new girl comes to the school, she tries to get in with the right crowd. You just don't give a damn, do you?"

"I never liked crowds," said Jill.

"You hang around with crowds, you get invited to parties," said David.

"Next year I'll party, when I'm in college," she told them. "This year my only goal is passing algebra."

"Did you have a test today?" asked Alan.

She nodded.

"How'd you do?"

"I copied all the problems from the girl next to me."

"You better hope she knew what she was doing."

"I figure in another week *I'll* know what I'm doing," said Jill.

"You pick it up fast," said Alan.

"Alan thinks you're smart," said Mark.

"Not a genius like him, but smart," said David.

"You're a genius?" Jill asked Alan.

He wasn't even embarrassed by the question. "I test high," is all he said.

"I thought geniuses were antisocial."

He grinned. "Not all of us."

Jill took a chance. "I thought geniuses were all intense and frustrated and suicidal."

If *suicidal* hit a note with any of them, they didn't show it. David just said, "Alan isn't even intense when he's pitching. I don't even think he cared there were scouts out there tonight."

"Why should I care?" asked Alan. "I'm not looking to be a ball player."

"What do you want to be?" asked Jill.

"A doctor, like my old man."

"Maybe you'll end up in Africa," she said.

"No way," said Alan. "I'm going in it for the bucks."

Jill gave it one more try. "I guess you're too practical to be suicidal."

"You got to be stupid to kill yourself," said Alan. "You only got one life, why waste it?"

They weren't picking up on it and she decided not to push it any further. It was puzzling, though. She would have thought a suicide in their school would have caused a lot of talk, a lot of speculation. Or maybe they knew it wasn't suicide at all.

"You ought to have a party over here," said David.

"Yeah, with no parents around to chaperone," said Mark.

"No parties," said Jill.

"Why not?"

"I'm not that sociable. Anyway, I don't want my aunt and uncle shipping me back to Africa."

"You don't mind if we stop by sometime, do you?" asked Alan.

"Not if you call first," said Jill.

"Then I guess you'll have to give me your phone number."

Jill wrote down her number and handed it to him. "Next time bring a pizza," she said. She must be getting lonely to be handing out her number to high school boys. For some reason, though, she was finding them good company. Probably because they were the only company she had.

"I HEAR SINGER pitched a no-hitter," said Trader before he even closed the door.

"Ummm," mumbled Doug.

"That must have been something. I wish I could've been there."

Doug tried to summon up even the semblance of excitement, but couldn't manage it. Instead he slumped further down in the chair and took another sip of his beer. "How'd the track meet go?"

"Not bad, although Jordan sprained his ankle in the pole vault. Come on, Dougie, tell me about the game. I hear there were scouts out there."

"Oh, yeah, the kid'll get offers. I don't think he's interested, though." And interest was one thing Doug could spot, since he had none himself.

"I wish I could've seen it," said Trader. "We have any beer?"

"There's a six-pack in the refrigerator."

He thought of Singer going up to Jill after the game and talking to her. He didn't like it. He didn't like it at all. Arrogant kid like that ought to stay away from the nice girls. There was something cold about Singer he didn't like. Either that or he was jealous of a high school kid, and that wasn't something he was about to admit.

Trader came back in the room and flipped on the TV. He couldn't seem to be in the house without background noise, even though he rarely looked at the screen unless there was some game in progress.

"Hey, come on, Lacayo, I want to hear about the game."

"You want a play-by-play description?"

"Yeah."

"Gimme a break, I'm tired."

"What do you say we get up early and drive down to the Keys?"

"To pick up women?"

"If you prefer, we can go fishing."

"I don't know, Woleski."

"What's the matter with you lately? You act like you're in love or something, but you can't be in love because you never even pick up women anymore."

"I need a career change."

"You need a woman."

"Maybe you're right," said Doug, not wanting to hear a lecture.

"So we'll drive to the Keys?"

"Why not?"

"We'll get an early start, get down there around noon."

"Fine."

"You can tell me about the game along the way." He reached for the remote control and flicked over the channels until he found a boxing match. The sound was turned up and Doug was able to relax.

What the hell he was doing coaching a baseball team, he didn't know. He hated baseball. He hated sports. When you grew up on the south side of Chicago, though, that wasn't something you admitted to. You either liked sports or you were a sissy, and being considered a sissy never had appealed to him.

Not that he hadn't liked sports as a kid. He had played sandlot baseball and followed the White Sox. He had made the football team in high school and went to the Bears games with his dad. It was just that, once he was in college, he began to lose his interest in sports. They seemed childish to him, something to do when you were a kid, but of little interest when you were grown. The trouble was, when you were with men, you either talked about sports or you were considered weird. So he talked sports, but he didn't enjoy it.

What he didn't understand was why he couldn't admit this to Trader. They'd been best friends for years and sometimes it made him feel like a fake. It was bad enough he didn't like picking up women; if he admitted to being bored by sports, there'd be nothing left of their friendship. And that would be too bad because he felt genuinely close to Trader.

He wondered what would happen if he got up, turned off the TV, and said, "You know something, Woleski? I hate sports."

But he couldn't quite get up his courage to do it.

Chapter Four

My prince looked at me today. I was wearing my
new pink mini with the matching top and had put
lots of gel in my hair to make it stand up. I guess it
worked. I got so nervous when he looked at me
that I dropped my books. Then *everyone* looked at
me. I almost died!!

JILL KNEW HER PROBLEM: she had no patience. Absolutely none. Show her a wrong to be righted, she wanted
it done yesterday. Give her a challenge, such as algebra, she wanted to master it instantly. Interest her in a
man and there was no way she was going to wait until
high school graduation to get to know him.

Maybe it was out of boredom, maybe it was out of
loneliness, maybe it was out of sheer perversity, but she
had it bad for Lacayo and it was getting worse by the
day.

It didn't help that she had no one to confide in. She
couldn't even drop by and see her parents because several high school students lived in their block and might
see her. Meeting them for dinner somewhere could re-
sult in the same thing. She had no friends in Palm Cove
and she couldn't afford long-distance calls to her friends

in Africa. And she missed them; she really missed them. She wouldn't have thought that she'd be homesick for Ethiopia, but she was. She missed the dry winds, the endless skies, the spectacular sunsets, the camaraderie with the other World Health workers, the feeling of accomplishing something worthwhile daily, even if it was only a drop in the bucket. She even missed speaking Amharic, which wasn't one of the easier languages to master.

And now, on a short leave of absence, for whatever reason, she was falling for him. Oh, she knew the signs, all right. The day brightened as soon as she saw him each morning, fell into shadows when he wasn't around. She was eating too much ice cream—for her a sure sign of frustration—and having trouble falling asleep at night. She found herself doodling variations of "Jill Lacayo" on her homework at night, then having to recopy it to hand it in. She had hated the weekend because it meant two long days of not seeing him at all. She had even looked for his number in the phone book with the pure intention of calling him and then hanging up at the sound of his voice. Luckily it wasn't listed or she might have made a real fool of herself. She knew the signs, and they were all present and accounted for. She also knew her lack of patience could get her in a lot of trouble, and she was beginning not to care. The entire thing was ridiculous anyway. Five minutes alone in his company and she might hate him. She'd sure like the opportunity to prove that thesis, though.

The arguments in civics escalated. If she couldn't date him, at least she could spar with him. Forget that her principles lay in ruins as she argued any side left open of any argument. If Lacayo saw black, she saw white, much to the amusement of the class. It was only when apartheid was broached that she backed down.

Lacayo looked directly at her. "No argument, Jill?"

"No."

"You mean you finally agree with me on something?"

"I'm afraid so," she said, to the laughter of her classmates.

"What if I took the opposite side?"

She shook her head. "No one could do that."

"Any takers?" he asked the class at large, but Jill didn't think they even knew what he was talking about. Anyway, Palm Cove practiced its own version of apartheid, to judge from the all-white student body.

Meanwhile Alan was showing a decided interest in her. She suddenly started seeing him in the halls all the time and he always called out to her. He had switched desks with David in civics so that he could more easily write notes to her, usually caustic remarks having to do with her arguments with Lacayo. In study hall he tutored her in algebra every day, and a couple of times he'd called her at home.

He didn't ask her out, though, and she was relieved by that, although dating even a high school boy was beginning to sound better than endless nights and weekends by herself. When she had first arrived back in the States, she had consumed all the television and books and magazines and newspapers at her disposal. There were programs on TV she had never heard of, magazines she had never seen, a new president she knew nothing about, new writers she hadn't read, rock stars she hadn't heard. But they no longer sufficed. It was adult company she craved now, and one adult in particular.

A couple of times she was ready to chuck the whole thing. Susan was dead, and finding out what happened wasn't going to change that. But then she would talk to her mother on the phone and knew that she had to keep going for her parents' sake. She could tell they still thought Susan had killed herself, despite what she'd found in the diary, and they were blaming themselves entirely.

Alan kept the phone calls friendly and amusing. The second time he called, she said, "Hey, Alan, don't you have a girlfriend?" She thought he might mention a former girlfriend who had died.

All he said, though, was, "No."

"What about David and Mark?"

"No girlfriends."

"What's with you guys, you gay?"

"Is that what you think?"

"It's a reasonable conclusion."

"Then why am I calling you?"

"That's what I'm wondering."

"We go to parties. We're just not much interested in the girls around here."

"What's the matter, did some girl dump you and break your heart?"

She could hear him laughing. "You trying to analyze me or something?"

"Or something."

"The last girl I went with was sophomore year and I dumped her. She was boring, okay?"

"Okay."

"What about you? Did you have a boyfriend in Africa?"

"Sure I did. I'm not weird like you."

"And?"

"And what?"

"Do you write him?"

"I wrote him once. I'll be going to college next year in the States, so I wouldn't be seeing him anymore anyway, except maybe on vacations."

"It doesn't sound serious."

"It wasn't. High school isn't supposed to be serious. I'll never understand those kids who take it so seriously they kill themselves." She got tears in her eyes just saying it, but she had to find out.

Alan didn't bite, though. Instead he changed the subject.

She didn't think Alan was the prince anyway. He was good-looking enough, but he didn't seem the type to get interested in her little sister. If he was getting interested in her it was only because she had the self-confidence that came from being ten years out of high school and he sensed a challenge. Coming into a new school, Susan no doubt lacked any confidence at all. Alan probably would've ignored her.

By Wednesday of her second week of school Jill knew she had Lacayo interested in her. He seemed to thrive on their arguments in class and he watched her and Alan like a hawk in study hall. She could tell it was unnerving him. The poor guy was probably wondering why he was attracted to a high school student. She also knew he'd deny it if asked, but there was no mistaking the look in his eyes when their arguments got heated. For a while they would seem all alone in the room, and then someone in the class would laugh or yell out something and the mood would be broken.

Well, if he was frustrated, she was twice as frustrated. She was getting nowhere in her investigation, she was overwhelmed with schoolwork, and she had no one to confide in. She had the thought—although maybe she was wrong—that if she confessed who she was to Lacayo, he would help her out. And while he helped her out, they could get to know each other.

She knew he liked her, if only as a student, and she didn't think he'd turn her in. And, oh, how nice it would be to have someone to talk to. And just maybe he had heard something she wasn't likely to hear. And just maybe she didn't care. To be entirely honest, wanting to confess to Lacayo had very little to do with Susan and a whole lot to do with the way Jill was feeling about him.

She knew she couldn't confront him at school. She thought of calling him at home, but she'd already tried to find his number and he hadn't been listed. She couldn't just walk into the school office and request his phone number, which is why she came up with the idea of following him home after school on Wednesday.

She thought of it in English and couldn't get it out of her mind the rest of the day. She knew she'd do it because once her mind was set on something she did it, even if it was foolish. By the time she got to P.E., she was counting off the minutes. It was during P.E., though, that she remembered he coached the baseball team and there would probably be practice after school.

The major problem this presented was that she'd have to wait until after he was finished with practice, which meant that the team would be coming out to the parking lot at the same time he would. And that meant Alan and the boys would surely see her car in the parking lot and come over to see what she was doing there. Alan wouldn't let something like that slip by unnoticed.

After school she scouted out the area. All the cars leaving the school headed west to a stop light before going in different directions. One corner held a service station, two corners had private residences, and the fourth had a small shopping center. Unfortunately, she didn't know what kind of car Mr. Lacayo drove. She'd just have to park in the shopping center and try to get a look at him in the car as he went by. If the sun reflected off the windows, she'd be out of luck.

It was a two-hour wait in a hot car, during which she consumed a lot of ice cream from the overpriced ice-cream parlor in the upscale shopping center and got a lot of fantasizing done.

"Mr. Lacayo? My name is really Jill Peters and I'm twenty-seven years old."

"Thank God! I knew I couldn't be falling in love with a student."

"You're falling in love with me?"

"From the first moment you walked into my class."

No, that wasn't correct. She had already been seated when he walked into class. And she really wasn't ready for protestations of love. She would rather build up to that slowly, add a little suspense.

Maybe: *"Mr. Lacayo? There's something I have to tell you."*

"I already know."

"You couldn't know."

"Look, I feel the same way, but there's nothing we can do about it until you graduate."

"Actually, there is."

"Are you eighteen already?"

"I'm twenty-seven."

A look of incredulity. *"And you're still in high school?"*

Well, she never had been very good at fantasies. And meanwhile she was dying of the heat and getting sticky from the ice cream. It never once crossed her mind, though, to give it up.

She tried thinking of culture shock, something she found herself experiencing several times each day. For one thing, driving here was a hassle. She was constantly having to stop for stop signs and red lights and missed the freedom of driving a four-wheel drive across the desert. Gas was cheaper, though, but that was the only thing that was. There wasn't much to spend money on where she was in Ethiopia, and she knew she was becoming something of a miser.

Another thing that bothered her was that people weren't friendly. No one smiled at her and said hello on the street, and some of the salespeople in the stores were downright rude. And she didn't think it was because they thought she was a teenager, because when she was alone she tended not to act like one.

She supposed she would have experienced culture shock just moving from Michigan to Palm Cove, but coming directly from Ethiopia was even worse. She had gone from the most desperate poverty to the most affluence she had ever seen. Palm Cove even made Saudi Arabia appear somewhat shabby. She had never seen so much wealth concentrated in one town and flaunted so openly. There had been a few rich families where she had grown up, but the rich people there had driven old station wagons and worn conservative clothes, not like the frivolous clothes she saw being worn here, most of which looked disposable.

Downtown Palm Cove was luxury taken to the limits. She had never seen such a concentration of expensive shops and was unused to seeing such an abundance of goods. The one time she had walked around down there, she had felt so out of place in the first store she had walked into, she walked right back out.

She was appalled at the waste of natural resources. It took her days to realize she could stand under a shower for more than sixty seconds and that she didn't have to recycle her dishwater. Even though it rained often enough to cause people's yards to resemble jungles, she still saw sprinkler systems automatically go on every morning.

Even the people's attitude toward the sun was different. In Africa, she wore a wide-brimmed straw hat and sunglasses when she was outdoors and found a shady spot to be in if at all possible. Here the people revelled in the sun no matter how high the temperature.

And if he didn't drive by soon, she was either going to die of the heat or have to find a shady spot to park.

IT WAS AFTER FIVE when she saw Alan's car speed by, running the light on the corner. She didn't know why she had thought she'd have trouble recognizing Lacayo's car. It was easy. It was the only one as old as hers. It was a light blue Datsun with a bent fender, a rusty door and a bumper sticker that said Ban Automatic Weapons. She bet that wasn't a popular sentiment around here.

She pulled out on the street and left two cars between them. She only hoped he didn't get on I-95 as she was sure she would lose him in rush-hour traffic.

It turned out he lived only a short distance from the school, and she was surprised to see what an expensive house it was. As he pulled up in the driveway, she kept driving and went around the block. She was beginning to have second thoughts. A single man would not be living alone in a house that size, which meant he probably had a wife. Maybe children. She felt miserable at the thought that she might have been flirting with a married man and angry at the thought he'd been flirting with her.

She kept driving around the block, wondering what to do. She finally decided to go through with it, anyway. If he was married, she'd rather find out now, and even if he was, that didn't mean he wouldn't keep her secret and help her. She felt as though she was stuck and had to try something, plus the suspense about his marital status was now driving her nuts.

She felt stupid parking in front of the house and walking up to the door. His wife might not appreciate mature students calling on her husband. On the other hand, maybe it was his parents' house. Just the thought calmed her down a little and it seemed to make sense. She didn't think a teacher, even with a working wife, could afford a house the size of the one she was standing in front of. But rich parents? Why not? Her parents had a nice house even though she wouldn't be able to afford one. She wasn't too thrilled with the idea of a grown man still living with his parents, but what the hell, no one was perfect. All fantasies of ever seeing him alone, though, would have to be discarded.

She rang the bell and waited. She heard a musical chime inside the house playing out a tune and found it annoying. When a servant in a uniform answered the door, she knew he couldn't be married. A teacher with a maid? It just wasn't possible.

"Is Mr. Lacayo home?" she asked the woman.

"Around the back," she was told.

"The back?"

"In the guest cottage. Just follow the driveway."

Jill grinned with relief and backed away from the door. A guest cottage? Fantastic! That was exactly the sort of place a single teacher would live. No parents, no wife—it was just going to be the two of them, alone, just the way she had planned it.

DOUG GOT OUT of the shower, wrapped a striped beach towel around his waist, and went into the kitchen. He grabbed two cans of beer out of the fridge and threw one to Trader. "Want to catch a movie tonight?" he asked him.

"What's playing?"

"What're you, a movie critic now? Who cares what's playing?"

"As long as it's not foreign," said Trader.

"When was the last time Palm Cove got a foreign film?"

"Not since I've lived here."

"Then what're you giving me a hard time about?"

"You know something, Doug? You're really getting argumentative lately."

"I know."

"If you were a woman I'd think—"

"I know what you'd think."

"We've only got a couple more months of school, why're you sweating it?"

"I'm argumentative in class, too."

"Just don't take it out on me, okay?"

Doug sat down at the table and was just opening up the paper to the movie section when someone knocked on the door.

"You paid the rent, didn't you?" asked Trader.

"Of course I paid it."

"Then who's that?"

"Why don't you open the door and find out?"

Trader left the room and a moment later Doug heard, "Hey, *Mr.* Lacayo, it's for you."

The *"Mr."* should have warned him, but it didn't. Not even thinking about the towel wrapped around his waist, Doug went into the living room. He couldn't believe it when he saw her standing in the doorway. She came *here*? Was she out of her *mind*?

"What are you doing here?" Doug asked her, hearing the panic in his voice as he said it.

"I have to talk to you," she said, and he had to give it to her, she didn't look in the least nervous. Trader, on the other hand, was looking floored.

Doug made an effort to sound professional when he said, "Make an appointment with me at school, Jill."

"School?" yelled Trader. "She's a *student*?"

"Take it easy, Woleski."

"Easy? You have a *student* coming to our house?"

Jill was looking a little less certain of herself. "I don't want to make an appointment; it's personal." She looked at Trader as though she thought he'd disappear at the news, but Trader was holding his ground.

"You've got a *student* visiting you?" Trader's voice had risen about an octave. "And you're standing there in a *towel*? Jesus, Lacayo, are you out of your mind?"

Doug belatedly remembered the towel and grabbed hold of it in case it might pick this exact moment to slip to the floor. At the very least it would give Trader a heart attack.

"If it's personal, Jill, the school has a good guidance counselor," he said, trying to sound as though he was fully clothed and in control.

Woleski was almost beside himself. "Get her out of here, man, before you get us fired."

"You're going to have to go," Doug told Jill.

She didn't back down. What's more, she looked amused. "It will only take a minute, Mr. Lacayo—"

"Please," he said, finding himself wishing that Trader were somewhere else and he could invite her in. This was exactly the kind of thinking that was going to get him fired. He couldn't understand what was the matter with himself.

She gave him a long, hard look, then glanced at Trader, who was now practically in tears. "All right," she said, sounding and acting a lot more adult than they were. "I'm sorry I bothered you," And with that she turned around and walked off down the driveway.

Doug was watching her retreat as Trader slammed the door shut and braced his back against it as though he thought she was going to come back and break her way in.

"I don't believe it," said Trader. "And you wearing a *towel*. Cool, Doug, real cool."

"You act like I invited her here," he said, knowing how defensive he sounded.

"I notice she knew where you lived. You handing out your address to students these days? No wonder you don't want to pick up women. You're seeing a high school girl."

"Get serious, Woleski. Did it sound like I'm seeing her? She wanted to talk to me, that's all."

"I hate to think what would've happened if I hadn't been here."

"Nothing would've happened. I probably would've looked out the window first and not even opened the door."

Trader gave him a doubtful look. "Who is she, anyway? I want to make sure she never takes one of *my* classes."

"She's the one I was telling you about. The one from Africa."

"The one who gives you all the arguments?"

Doug nodded. "There's something about her, I don't know...."

"She's a kid, for God's sake."

"She doesn't seem like a kid."

"I think you better get out of teaching, Lacayo, and the sooner the better."

"Will you calm down? Come on, let's finish our beers."

"I can't believe you just walked out half-naked."

"You didn't exactly announce who it was."

"Forget the movies tonight," said Trader. "We're going to go to a singles bar and you're going to meet someone your own age."

"I'm telling you, Trader, it's not like that."

"And I'm telling you, you're lucky if it stops here. It's bad news when a student gets a crush on you. Next she'll be calling you up, sending you notes, trying to get you alone in school. I've seen it happen to better teachers than you, Doug."

"She's not like that."

"Then why'd she come here?"

"I'll be damned if I know."

"Just watch it, buddy. Cover yourself."

"You mean like this?" asked Doug, letting the towel drop to the floor as he turned to moon Trader.

"You think it's all a joke? Wait till her father shows up some night with a shotgun."

"Her father's in Africa."

"You hope!"

OH, GOD, she'd made a fool of herself. A complete and utter fool. Doug. Douglas Lacayo. What a great name! God, she felt stupid. What an idiot she had been. At least it hadn't been a woman with him.

The panic in his eyes. She didn't think she'd ever forget the sheer panic in his eyes when he saw her. And the other guy, of course, was totally freaking out. What was the big deal, a student dropping by? You would've thought by their reactions that it was the end of the world.

It was kind of funny, come to think of it. Mr. Lacayo in a bright, multicolored, striped beach towel and his hair plastered to his head. Just what she needed to see, the object of her affections half-naked and sexy as hell. She'd never get to sleep tonight.

She could've blurted it out. She could've said, "Hey, guys, I'm just a fake student. I'm really your age." She had somehow sensed, however, that it wasn't the right moment. It probably would've taken the roommate two seconds to get on the phone to the principal and that would have been the end of her charade.

A woman with any sensibility at all would be embarrassed beyond belief and never show up at school the next day. Too bad. She felt she had conducted herself properly; it wasn't her fault Lacayo panicked so easily. In fact she couldn't wait to see the expression on his face in civics tomorrow. She'd bet anything he wouldn't start another argument in class. She had a feeling she'd scared the hell out of him.

Not a bad body at all. Big shoulders; nice pecs; firm stomach, what she'd been able to see of it; legs a little bowed, which might account for his sexy walk. There was a prince in civics all right—it was just that she wasn't in agreement with Susan over who it was.

She'd have to search the diary for more clues tonight; she wasn't getting anywhere. She had a feeling Phaedra knew something, but she wasn't talking. Maybe what Phaedra needed was to be forced down to the police station and scared into talking. And as a last resort, Jill would do that.

She looked with longing at every bar she passed on the way home. What she wouldn't give to be able to walk in, order a drink and relax with some adult company. That was probably why when Alan called to see if he could stop by, she said yes. At least he was intelligent and about the closest to adult company she was going to get for a while.

When he showed up he was carrying a six-pack. "Do you mind?" he asked, holding it up.

So she was contributing to the delinquency of a minor, so what? "I could use a couple of beers," she told him.

His eyes lit up for a moment, as though he was under the impression a couple of beers would get her drunk. This kid had a lot to learn.

He helped her with her algebra and when they were finished she thought she could finally cope with what they were on in class.

"Thanks," she said. "I would've flunked without you."

"No way," he said. "You catch on faster than anyone I've ever seen."

"I always liked math."

"Me too. It makes more sense than any of the other subjects."

She got up from the table and turned on the TV to MTV, then opened them each the last of the beers. "I ought to pay you for tutoring me."

"No charge."

"How about if I send out for a pizza?"

"Food I'll accept."

They watched the music videos until the pizza arrived, then she decided to do a little further detective work. This time, however, it was personal.

"You have a game this weekend?" she asked him.

"Yeah. Friday night, in Miami. You coming?"

"I doubt it."

"I don't blame you."

"I didn't realize Mr. Lacayo was also a coach."

"He tries," said Alan.

"You win, don't you?"

"I love the way you two argue in class. Plus it lets the rest of us off the hook."

"You mean you don't read the newspaper?"

"What for?"

"To find out what's going on in the world."

"Who cares?"

"I think you care more than you pretend."

Alan ignored that.

"Does Lacayo coach anything else?"

"No, just baseball. Woleski coaches everything else."

"Who's Woleski?"

"He's head of the P.E. department."

"Do I know him?"

"You've probably seen him around. Big guy, going bald, but he's not all that old."

The image of Lacayo's roommate flashed in her mind. "Bushy mustache?"

"Yeah, that's him."

"So tell me something, Alan. Is it always this boring in Palm Cove? Doesn't anything exciting ever happen around here?"

"I guess that depends on your idea of excitement."

"The place seems dead to me."

"Then come to our game in Miami. It's a little more lively down there. Most of our parents moved here from there so there wouldn't be any excitement around for us."

"That's too bad."

"Listen, it's a good school academically, and that's all I care about. I just want to get into med school."

She gave him a challenging look. "Are you the model student you pretend to be?"

He shrugged expansively. "I'm not pretending to be anything. I *am* a model student."

"And I'm Benazir Bhutto."

"Who?"

Jill shook her head. "What do I have to do to get some stimulating conversation around here?"

Alan just smiled.

JILL READ SOME MORE of Susan's diary in bed that night, then made a list of all the dark-haired boys in her civics class. There were fourteen of them. In fact every boy in the class with the exception of David had dark hair. And most of them could be considered good-looking. One, Jackie Lenier, was a total nerd, and she crossed him off her list. She didn't think even a high school girl could conceivably consider Jackie to be a prince.

The rest of them she'd question Phaedra about. Just whether they had girlfriends, what they were like, the innocuous kinds of questions that a new girl might be expected to ask about boys. One of them knew something about her sister but she didn't know how to get that information short of seducing every boy in the class in the hopes of dragging it out of him. And even the thought of it was a drag because the only one she'd really like to seduce was the teacher.

On that frustrating note, she turned off the light and slid down in the bed. She hoped Lacayo was as wide awake at two in the morning as she was. It would serve him right.

DOUG WAS WIDE AWAKE and wondering what was the matter with him. Why in hell, after years of teaching high school girls, was he suddenly going off the deep end over one? What on earth was so special about her? The school was filled with gorgeous, nubile blondes in sexy little outfits, and all he could focus on was one slim blonde who dressed like a boy.

Not that she didn't look good; she looked just fine. He imagined her short haircut was eminently practical in Africa and she didn't need any makeup. She had intelligent eyes, a nose about a third the size of his, a wide mouth with a smile that sometimes mocked him, a small chest, and long legs; in short, nothing to lose his head over. And yet there was something about her that was driving him nuts and it wasn't just her argumentative nature, either. There was an intelligence there, but lots of the students were intelligent. She was different from the other girls, but nothing that couldn't be explained by missionary parents in Africa.

It had to be burnout, there was no other logical explanation. He was truly tired of teaching, he hated coaching baseball, and while he dearly loved Trader, he longed for more stimulating conversation than the scores of the ball games and Trader's scores with women. There was a whole world out there, and he was stuck in a dead-end job in a dead-end town.

It was time to make some changes, but meanwhile, beginning tomorrow morning, he'd start cooling it toward Jill. He was obviously encouraging her with the arguments in class, so that would have to stop. He wouldn't smile at her, he wouldn't speak to her, she'd become the invisible student. And maybe he'd take Trader's advice and get out and start meeting some women. Not the kind that hung out in bars, but there must be other places to meet them. Somewhere there must be an intelligent woman who wouldn't mind his company.

A woman of at least voting age.

Chapter Five

My prince has dark hair and eyes, which I think go perfectly with my blond hair and blue eyes. If we had the same coloring we'd look like brother and sister, and that wouldn't be interesting. He smiled at me in class today and I could've died of happiness. I was so surprised, I didn't think to smile back. I think that's just as well, as this way I appeared cool. It never hurts to play a little hard to get. But if he smiles at me tomorrow, I've decided to smile back.

DOUG COULDN'T BELIEVE he was apprehensive about going to school and facing a student. Couldn't believe that some high school senior had him intimidated. He came very close to calling in sick. Only the fact that postponing the meeting for a day wasn't going to solve things finally got him in his car and on his way.

He decided to ignore her. He'd pretend she wasn't there, look through her as though she were invisible. That ought to cool her ardor, or whatever it was she was feeling. He'd been too friendly to her, that was the problem. Sure she was the brightest one in the class, or at least the only one who ever read the newspapers and knew what was going on in the world. Sure she was fun to argue with, and it made the class go by quickly. Sure he was attracted to her, but that attraction in itself was unseemly, and if he got fired for that kind of conduct, it would reflect on his friend, Trader, who had been instrumental in getting him the job.

It had to be boredom. It was hating the teaching job, hating Palm Cove, wanting a change in his life, wanting to spend his time with adults for a change instead of kids. He was bored out of his skull—that was the problem. Otherwise, what was he doing thinking about a high school girl?

By the time he walked into his 10:25 civics class he felt in control again. He didn't even glance at the back of the room where he knew she'd be seated. He took the roll call head down, broached the topic of the day, which was airline deregulation, and waited for her clear voice of reason to enter into the dispute.

It didn't happen.

After ten fruitless minutes of trying to interest the class in something that was of no interest to them whatsoever, he switched over to ethics in government. He figured this was something Jill could surely sink her teeth into, but not only didn't she bite, the rest of the class looked ready for sleep. Some of them were already asleep.

"Hey, let's wake up in here and smell the coffee," he said, but it didn't even get a smile.

If he didn't know better, he'd think she was absent. Maybe she was feeling even more embarrassed at showing up at his house than he was. He sneaked a look at the back row, and there she was brazening it out. What's more, she seemed to be writing notes back and forth to Alan Singer. He could be in another classroom for all she seemed to care.

Well, fine. Great. That's what he wanted, wasn't it? She'd given up whatever had been on her mind the day before, and that was swell with him. He didn't personally see the attraction of Alan Singer, but then he wasn't a high school girl, was he?

He reached for his old standby, violence on TV, and when that didn't quite shake them up, he moved into violence on music videos. If anything got a discussion out of the class, that was the subject.

Pure apathy. Most of the class now openly focussed their attention on the clock. He could almost hear their little minds counting off the seconds.

"Take out your pencils and paper," he said. "We're going to have a quick quiz."

That woke them up all right and he smiled as the groans grew in volume. He made up the test off the top of his head, using subjects they'd discussed in class during the semester. He wrote out fifteen questions on the board, each requiring a one-sentence answer, then sat down at his desk and watched them at work.

If you could call it work. A few of them seemed to be writing; more seemed to be faking it. Now *he* started watching the clock, thinking that forty minutes could be interminable when you weren't having fun.

The bell for the end of the period managed to shake them out of their lethargy, and as they quickly filed out the door, they dropped off their tests on his desk. He scanned them, finding mostly blank papers. Except for one. One had every answer correct; it also went further than required and brought up points he wouldn't have dared put on the test.

Jill's of course. And even without acknowledging his presence, even without arguing against him, she was still getting to him, much as he disliked admitting it. He would have liked to think he had taught her a lesson, but he'd be damned if he knew just what lesson that was.

JILL FELT a little sorry for Lacayo. The poor guy had looked flustered, had made a big effort to ignore her, had then switched gears and tried to involve her in an argument. She was the one who should have been embarrassed, but he had acted so embarrassed that hers had faded away. Maybe she ought to write him a letter and explain things. Then again, maybe she ought to leave him alone and get on with her investigation.

During civics she had listed all the dark-haired boys' first and last names when roll was called. Alan had noticed her doing it and asked why in a note.

"Maybe I'm interested in them," she wrote back.

"*All* of them?"

"Why not?"

"Even Jackie?"

"Well, no, not Jackie." Jackie definitely was not the prince.

"Good luck!" wrote Alan, finding it all highly amusing.

Then Lacayo had sprung the test and she had almost laughed out loud. She could tell she was the only one busily writing out the answers, but she loved it. It was almost as good as talking to him. It might even be better, since he couldn't argue back. She was tempted to write a little personal note to him at the end, but in the interests of not causing him to have a heart attack, she desisted.

Now if she could only do as well on an algebra test, she'd be in business.

AT LUNCH Jill asked Phaedra if she'd go to the mall with her Friday night.

"You going to get some new clothes?" asked Phaedra.

Jill looked down at her jeans. "You think I need 'em, huh?"

"Well..."

"Maybe one skirt."

"You'd look great in a miniskirt," said Phaedra.

"We could get something to eat and maybe go to a movie afterward."

Phaedra looked as thrilled as though someone had asked her to a school dance.

Oddly enough, Jill was beginning to feel peer pressure to conform. Forget that they weren't her peers; she was still feeling it. She was getting tired of being viewed as the odd girl out.

Somehow she wasn't doing all that well in her student impersonation, either. The hardest thing to adjust to was being treated like a child. She hadn't liked being treated like a child when she was a child, and she liked it a whole lot less as an adult.

She kept messing up the little things. In most classes—Lacayo's was the exception—students were supposed to raise their hands before speaking, but Jill was constantly speaking up and getting chastised for it. She had started speaking to her Spanish teacher as an equal one day and didn't stop until she finally noticed how uncomfortable the woman was becoming.

She was finding it difficult to concentrate in class, resented homework assignments and longed for some good adult conversation.

She was also gaining weight on the cafeteria food.

THE MALL WAS spectacular: three department stores plus a myriad of shops, two restaurants, four fast-food places and eight different movies being shown concurrently at one theater. There hadn't been anything like it in her hometown in Michigan.

Phaedra had been so insistent on Jill's buying some clothes that in order to pacify her, she found herself trying on miniskirts in several stores. She finally bought one, mostly because it was made out of blue denim and didn't look much different than cutoff jeans. And she had to admit it would be a lot cooler. She finally managed to wean Phaedra away from the clothes by announcing she was starving. Phaedra, who was always starving, led the way to her favorite restaurant.

Jill began her investigation over cheeseburgers by questioning Phaedra about the boys on her list. Mostly she wanted to find out if they had girlfriends.

Phaedra proved to be a font of knowledge on the dating habits of every boy in their class. Of the thirteen possible princes in civics, five were going steady and had been for over a year; four dated around but didn't have a current girlfriend; two—Alan and Mark—weren't sociable, and the rumor was they probably dated girls from other schools; one was interested only in computers and the chess club; and one, in Phaedra's opinion, was possibly gay.

Jill made note of the four possibles: Greg, Barry, John and Peter. They'd be the best place to start.

She tried to get more details about them from Phaedra, but didn't find out anything particularly helpful.

"Why are you so interested in them?" Phaedra asked at one point.

"Maybe I feel like dating," said Jill.

"What about your boyfriend in Africa?"

"Well, I'll be going away to college next year, anyway."

Phaedra gave her a commiserating look. "He hasn't written, huh?"

"Once. A postcard." She tried to look downcast.

"What about Alan? He seems interested in you."

"Oh, Alan," said Jill, dismissing him. "We're just friends."

"He's a cold fish, all right."

"No, I like Alan. I just don't like him the way you like a boyfriend."

"Yeah, I know what you mean," said Phaedra.

"I think I'm going to call them up and ask them out," said Jill, wondering what kind of response this would elicit.

Phaedra's eyes came wide awake. "You wouldn't dare!"

"Why not? Women have equal rights these days."

"You sound just like my mother." Phaedra's hand was snaking in the direction of Jill's French fries, so she slid them over to her.

"Do you think it'll shake them up?" she asked.

"If you want my opinion, I think they'll have heart attacks. I don't think girls ever ask boys out here."

"Well, I'm going to give it a try."

"Let me know if it works. Maybe I'll try it."

"What's the worst that can happen, they'll avoid me in school? We'll be out in a couple of months, anyway.

And it won't hurt my reputation, because I haven't been here long enough to have one."

"You have one," Phaedra assured her.

"I do?"

"Most of the boys like you and most of the girls don't."

"Well, that works out just fine because that's exactly the way I feel about them."

"Some of the girls think you're fast."

"Me?"

"I heard Marla telling her friends that she's sure you aren't a virgin. She thinks you're too self-confident to be a virgin, but I notice she claims to be one and she's about as self-confident as you can get."

Jill had to laugh. "Marla thinks I'm not a virgin? Innocent little me?"

"I don't think Marla and her friends are virgins, either, if you want to know the truth."

"In Africa they'd have a couple of kids by now."

"That's a scary thought," said Phaedra, but Jill could tell she was intrigued by the thought.

"Well, they're really going to think I'm fast when they hear I'm calling up boys and asking them out. You better watch it, Phaedra, I might ruin your reputation along with mine."

"I don't care," said Phaedra. "I'd love to get a bad reputation for something. It's better than having no reputation."

"Hang in there—things will get better in college."

"How do you know?"

Good question.

Trader casually threw out, "There's this singles bar I heard about in Delray Beach. I thought we could check it out tonight."

"Forget it," said Doug.

"Listen, I hear a lot of professional women go there."

"Which profession are you referring to?"

"I mean it. Business women. Maybe even lawyers."

"I doubt that they're looking to meet schoolteachers, Woleski."

"You don't know that."

"Let's just go to a movie."

"The only person I meet in a movie is you."

"Greg? This is Jill Wyckoff, I'm in civics with you."

"Hi."

"Hi. I was wondering if you wanted to go to a movie tonight."

"A movie?"

"Yes."

"With you?"

"That's right."

"Uhhhhhh . . ."

"Or we could do something else if you'd rather."

"Are you asking me out?"

"Yes."

"This has never happened to me."

"I'm sorry."

"Don't be sorry. I'm just surprised, that's all. Is that how it'd done in Africa?"

"Sure. Don't they do it that way here?"

"Not that I know of."

"So you want to go?"

"I don't want to hurt your feelings, but I can't."

"Oh, okay."

"I already have a date. I suppose I could break it..."

"No, don't do that. We can do it another time."

"You mean you'll call me again?"

"Sure."

"Well, thanks. Thanks a lot."

TRADER WAS BEGINNING to look beleaguered. "Well, what kind of a woman are you looking for?"

"I'm not looking."

"If you were."

Doug sighed. "You're not going to give up, are you?"

"Listen, you need a little change of pace that's all. You spend all week with kids, you coach a bunch of jocks, you need to meet some women."

"I'm glad you have my best interests at heart, Woleski."

"Okay, then how about this—why don't we join a health club?"

"You don't think we work out enough now?"

"Not to work out. To meet women. I hear that's where they all are these days."

"That's pretty expensive just to meet a woman."

"Then *you* think of something."

"BARRY?"

"Yeah?"

"This is Jill Wyckoff, from civics."

"How're you doin', Jill?"

"Fine. Listen, I was wondering if you'd want to go out tonight."

"Come again?"

"I'm asking you for a date, Barry."

"Why me?"

She tried to remember which one he was, but couldn't. "Why not you?"

"We've never talked, have we?"

"I figured we could talk on the date."

"You always do things like this?"

"Absolutely. All the time."

"I don't like it."

"Well, I'm sorry."

"I mean, if I wanted to go out with you, I'd ask you."

"Well, thanks anyway."

"I'll think about it, though. Maybe I'll give you a call sometime."

"I'll be waiting breathlessly."

"You got a phone number?"

Jill hung up on him.

"I'VE MANAGED to live my whole life without ever going to a country-western bar," Doug said. "I'm not going to start now."

"The thing is," said Trader, "they're real friendly places. Everyone dances with everyone else and they do this dance step that even you could learn."

"I can dance."

"You call that dancing? I've seen people being electrocuted who have more rhythm."

"You're not exactly Baryshnikov."

"So what do you say, you wanna give it a try?"

"I don't own any cowboy boots."

"Is JOHN HOME?"

"No, he's not. May I ask who's calling, please?"

"I'm a friend of his."

"John is with his father in Orlando this weekend."

"Oh."

"Would you like his number there?"

"No, that's okay. I'll talk to him in school."

"May I tell him who called?"

"No, that's not necessary. Thanks."

"ALL RIGHT," said Doug, "if it'll get you off my back, we'll go the bar in Delray."

"Way to go, Dougie!"

"I'm not promising anything."

"I'm not asking for anything. Save your promises for the women."

"I don't see why we can't just—"

"You'll have a great time, I promise."

"PETER?"

"Yes?"

"This is Jill Wyckoff, from civics."

"You callin' to ask me out?"

"What makes you think that?"

"Barry just called and said you asked him for a date."

"Oh."

"Go on, ask me."

"You're probably busy tonight."

"No I'm not."

"It's kind of late."

"Listen, just give me twenty minutes and I'll be ready. If I don't have to take a shower, I can be ready in ten."

"Go ahead, take a shower."

"Where're we going?"

"I thought maybe a movie."

"Great. You picking me up?"

"No problem."

"You paying?"

"Listen, do you even know who I am?"

"Sure I know. You're the one who always gives La-cayo a hard time."

"Right."

JUST FROM a quick glance Doug estimated that there were five women to every man in the bar. Out of those five, four didn't remotely resemble professional women. The others were marginal. "It looks like we have some competition," he said to Trader.

"No problem."

The men, on the other hand, looked professional. He and Trader were dressed in jeans and clean shirts; most of the men were wearing jackets and ties. "We're really going to impress those professional women."

"Women love jocks—always have, always will."

The smoke obscured the details, but Doug could make out an old-fashioned jukebox and a moose head over the bar. "What is this, a nostalgia bar?"

"What are you, an interior decorator?"

Trader led the way through the crowd to the bar and ordered them both a beer. Doug checked out some of the women at closer range. None seemed to be check-ing out him. Trader, though, was already getting some glances. He never had been able to figure out how Trader did it, but whatever he had, it was potent.

"Don't turn around," said Trader in a low voice, "but there are two petite brunettes by the jukebox al-most falling out of their tops." Trader was partial to petite brunettes, particularly if they had Spanish ac-cents and big chests.

Doug took a long swallow of beer and began to wish he'd stayed at home.

"You're not looking," said Trader.

"I'm not interested."

"Okay, stay here, I'll try to herd them over in this direction."

Doug knew when he heard the burst of laughter from the direction of the jukebox that Trader had struck gold.

PETER WAS CHECKING out her legs in the miniskirt, which was distracting Jill's eyes from the road. Any guy who came on this strong wasn't her idea of a prince. Still and all, it beat sitting home another Saturday night. Maybe if she played her cards right, he'd ask her to the senior prom.

"So, Jilly, you do a lot of dating in Africa?"

"It was more parties than anything else."

"A party girl, huh?"

"Well, there weren't any movies and the school was too small to have dances. We mostly just took turns having parties."

"I could get into that," said Peter.

"What movie do you want to see?"

"Who cares? Who's going to be watching the movie?"

She almost laughed out loud. The little punk thought he was going to make out, did he? "In that case, I'd like to see that new comedy with Goldie Hawn."

"Just as long as we sit in the back. I see better from a distance."

Right.

SALLY, WHO CLAIMED to be thirty but looked more like forty, was rubbing her leg up against Doug's beneath the table.

"So what do you do for a living, Doug, if I might ask?"

"I'm a teacher."

Sally winked at him. "I've heard about you college professors."

"I teach high school."

"I hated high school."

"I'm not crazy about it myself."

Sally leaned over to give him a better view down her blouse. "So tell me, does it drive you crazy being around all those cute little high school girls all day?"

Doug looked over at Trader for help, but Trader was whispering in Donna's ear. He felt like telling her, *Actually, there's one in particular who is driving me up the wall. And I have a feeling I have more in common with her than with you.* Instead he asked, "What do you do, Sally?"

"I work for the government."

"Doing what?"

"Anything they pay me to do," she said, then burst into laughter for no discernible reason. She reached over and squeezed Doug's thigh and he choked on his beer. Jill was pretty brazen, but he was reasonably sure she wouldn't do something like that.

PETER'S ARM was around the back of her seat even before the lights went down. When the theater was finally in darkness, she felt his hand move down to her shoulder and pause there. So he had his arm around her, big deal. It wasn't anything to make a fuss about. When his fingers began to walk across her chest, though, she took his hand and removed it.

"Hey, what's the problem?" Peter whispered in her ear.

"Try that again and I'll break your fingers."

"You don't mean that."

"Try me."

Peter relaxed for about ten minutes, then Jill felt his fingers, moving more slowly this time, begin to inch across her collar bone.

"What do you think I am, the school slut?" she hissed at him.

"Hey, no, listen, I really respect you."

"Then quit trespassing!" She said that loudly enough that the people in front of them turned around to stare.

When he removed his arm from around her shoulders and instead took her hand, she thought she had reformed him. When he placed her hand in his lap, however, she snatched it away and moved as far away from him as possible. What was really annoying her was that she had wanted to see the movie. For a fleeting moment she found herself wondering how Lacayo behaved on a date.

"YOU WANNA DANCE?" Sally asked him.

"I'm not much of a dancer," said Doug, not wanting to get that close to her.

"Hey, for this kind of dancing, all you've got to do is sway to the beat."

"Okay," said Doug, thinking it couldn't be any worse than having her move her hand along his thigh the way she was doing.

It was worse. She pressed against him so closely that he felt suffocated. He liked women. Hell, he liked them a lot. But he didn't like Sally, and no amount of pressing against him was going to change that fact. She was too obvious, she was too boring, and her perfume was just about asphyxiating him. And deep down he had really been hoping that he'd be attracted to some woman so he could prove to himself it wasn't high school girls he went for. Or at least one in particular.

"I'm really glad I came here tonight," said Sally.

"It's a nice place."

"You wouldn't believe the men you meet in places like this who come on to you. But you're a real gentleman." She gave a little thrust of her pelvis at the word *gentleman*.

Doug tried to put some distance between them.

JILL TOOK PETER OUT for a hamburger after the show. She still needed to question him, and she didn't want to leave because she had a feeling that she was going to be fighting him off in the car.

At least he didn't squeeze into the booth next to her. The place they went to was filled with high school kids, and Jill saw that they were getting a lot of looks.

"You weren't very friendly in the movie," Peter complained, but he waited until they had ordered their food before complaining, she noticed.

"It was a little public there, Peter," she said, giving him the impression that things would pick up when she took him home.

"I get you," he said, his eyes going to half mast in what she was sure he thought was a sexy look. Well, maybe it would be a sexy look to another teenager.

"I'm surprised you didn't already have a date tonight."

"I was just going to hang out with the guys."

"No girlfriend?"

"Not at the moment, but who knows?"

"I thought everyone went steady in high school."

"I don't like to get that serious," said Peter.

"You've never been serious about a girl?"

"Not particularly."

The subject seemed to be making Peter nervous, so Jill said, "Yeah, I guess high school is a little young to get serious. I mean, love and angst and suicide can all wait until you're older."

He looked at her as though she were crazy, and she couldn't blame him. "What's angst?" he asked.

"I don't know. I just made it up."

"You're a little weird, you know it?"

"I know. That's what my shrink says."

"You see a shrink?"

"Sure, don't you?"

He just shook his head, looking bewildered.

"Sometimes I feel suicidal," she confided in him, hoping the news wouldn't be all over school on Monday.

"Jeez."

"Don't you?"

"Uh-uh. Sometimes I feel like killing my father, but not really seriously. I mean, it just lasts a moment or two. Well, once it lasted a week, but that's because he grounded me."

"Actually, a high percentage of high school students commit suicide," said Jill, hoping against hope that he would say something about her sister.

"You're not going to try anything tonight, are you?"

"No, I feel great tonight."

For some reason, Peter didn't look relieved.

TRADER PRACTICALLY shoved him into the men's room. "Listen, I'm going home with Donna."

"Good luck," said Doug.

"The thing is, they came in the same car. You don't mind taking Sally home, do you?"

"Would it matter if I did?"

"What's the matter with you? You've got it in the bag."

"I don't like her, Woleski."

"What's not to like?"

"If you like her so much, take them both home. Have a threesome."

"What do you think, I'm kinky?"

Doug knew he was stuck. "I'll drive her home, okay?"

"Great. I'll see you sometime tomorrow."

How he was going to take that barracuda home and get out of there in one piece was worrisome.

"A FRIEND OF MINE committed suicide in Africa," said Jill, wishing she could think of a more subtle approach.

"No kidding!"

"Yeah. For no reason. Well, I guess he had a reason, but he didn't even leave a note."

"Could I have those fries if you're not going to eat them?"

Jill passed them over. "Did you ever know anyone who committed suicide?"

"A girl in our school not too long ago, but I didn't know her."

Now that she had gotten somewhere, she found she wasn't prepared for the sudden emotion she was feeling. She just hoped she wouldn't suddenly start crying. She swallowed and asked, "Was she a friend of yours?"

"Nah. She was in civics with me, but I never even talked to her. Of course I never talked to you before tonight, either."

"What was she like?"

Peter shrugged. "Quiet. I don't know. I hardly even noticed her."

"Her boyfriend must have felt terrible."

"I don't think she had one. She was new, kind of kept to herself."

She would swear he wasn't lying. What's more, she had a hard time believing any relative of hers would consider this bozo to be a prince.

"You know what I'd love?" said Jill.

"If it has to do with suicide, I don't think I want to hear it."

"Sorry about that. I'm not usually morbid. No, what I'd really love is a banana split. I don't think I've had one since I was sixteen."

"Gee, a whole year, huh?"

Another foul. "It seems like a long time."

"You going to buy me one, too?"

"You can have anything you want, Peter."

He grinned at her. "Hold that thought!" She knew if Lacayo had said that to her she'd melt on the spot. With Peter it was all she could do not to burst out laughing.

SHE WAS ALL OVER HIM in the car. What's more, the smell of her perfume was probably permanently imbedded in the upholstery. And just his luck, she lived in the opposite direction from him. He was not only going to miss *Saturday Night Live*, he might even miss *Face to Face* in the morning.

It got worse when he finally pulled up in front of her apartment complex. He got out of the car to walk her to the door and she backed him into the fender and lifted her face for a kiss.

"Look, Sally, I'm not really into this tonight."

"You sick or something?"

"Yeah, I think I'm coming down with the flu." That ought to do it. No one wanted to catch the flu.

"I got just the thing for you. We'll have some brandy and then get under my electric blanket."

"It's got to be eighty outside."

"I'll put the air-conditioning on."

"Not tonight, Sally, okay? I really feel beat."

Sally grabbed him by the hand and headed for the building. "How about a massage? I give great massages. I've even got this oil that smells like magnolias."

"Is that what your perfume is?"

"You recognized it? It's kind of my trademark."

At her door she grew pouty when he wouldn't go inside. "You mean you're just going to drop me off and go home?"

"Maybe another time."

"You wasted my whole night. You weren't the only man in the bar, you know."

"I know, and I apologize."

"Right now Donna's probably having a good time, and you're dumping me."

She was perhaps the most obnoxious woman he had ever met. "If you want to know the truth, Sally, you're not my type."

"What's your type, some high school cheerleader?"

Instant guilt.

PETER HAD HIS HAND on her knee and it didn't seem worth the effort to fight him off while she was driving.

"I hear you have your own apartment," he said, his voice kind of a strange growl.

"That's right."

"You going to show it to me?"

"Not tonight, Peter."

"What do I have to do, ask *you* out to see it? Want to go out tomorrow night?"

"I have too much homework."

"What're you pulling?"

"Nothing."

"You come on strong and then—"

"Come on strong? What're you talking about?"

"You call me up, you ask me out—that's what I'm talking about."

"You're not behaving right, Peter."

"Me?"

"You're too easy. You're supposed to play a little hard to get on a first date. Don't you read *Seventeen* magazine?"

"You pulling my leg?"

"A kiss at the door on a first date, that's all. Anything else and you'll get a bad reputation."

"I don't mind getting a bad reputation."

"With your mouth closed."

"You're the weirdest girl I ever met."

"Then, after the kiss, I say, 'I'll call you tomorrow,' and you spend all day tomorrow sitting by the phone and hoping it will ring."

"I'm going to the beach tomorrow."

"And then you start writing my name all over your notebook."

"I think you're from another planet."

Jill pulled up in front of his house and parked. "Now I walk you to the door."

"Oh, no," said Peter, lunging for her across the front seats. One kiss wouldn't kill her, she decided, but she kept her mouth firmly shut as his lips pressed down on hers. When his hands started to explore, though, she got the door of the car open and ducked out of his arms.

"Come on, Peter. Time to say good-night."

"What kind of a tease are you, anyway?"

"Get out before I start honking the horn and wake up your parents."

He got out and slammed the door. She didn't bother walking him to the door, but she waited until he went inside. He didn't say a word to her. He was sulking. Serves him right, she thought. Maybe next time he'd know how to behave on a date.

And maybe one of these days she could date a grown-up for a change.

Chapter Six

He said hi to me today! I tried to look surprised, to pretend I didn't care. I said hi back but I made it sound indifferent. Some of the girls looked jealous when he spoke to me. I think they all have crushes on him. After civics, the whole day seems boring.

DOUG SHOVED the clothes into the dryer, put in his quarters, then headed back to the Sunday papers he had left in the faded orange molded-plastic chair. God, he hated doing laundry. Another boring Sunday, but at least he hadn't woken up beside Sally this morning. It would be hard to imagine a worse way to wake up on a weekend than in bed with someone you didn't care about.

He was just congratulating himself on getting out of that one alive when *she* walked in. He took one look at her and felt his blood run hot, then cold.

"Hello, Mr. Lacayo." She sounded calm as you please and wore short-shorts that showed off her long legs and a white T-shirt with some kind of strange writing on it that resembled Arabic.

He looked around, sure that everyone in the laundromat was watching them. Watching what would look like a planned meeting between a teacher and one of his students. At the very least he expected the vice cops to burst through the door and arrest him.

He turned back to Jill, who was now smiling at him, all innocence, as though they met every day in the laundromat. He tried to maintain a semblance of calm, but it didn't work, and he ended up blurting out, "What're you doing here?"

She held up a stuffed pillowcase and a box of Tide. "Washing my clothes."

Okay, you ask a stupid question . . .

Only it didn't make sense. He had never run into a student at the laundromat. High school students didn't go to laundromats. Palm Cove students had maids who did that kind of thing. But then nothing about her seemed to make sense. He managed to lower his voice and ask in a doubtful tone, "You wash your own clothes?"

"I make my own bed, too. I'm not a child."

At the word *bed*, Doug felt himself blushing. He turned away from her, sure that everyone was listening, but most of the customers had gone back to their newspapers.

He turned back to her and whispered, "How did you know where I lived?"

She grinned. "I followed you home."

In his worst dreams . . .

"Did you follow me here, too?"

"I think you're paranoid, Mr. Lacayo," she said, going over to one of the washing machines and starting to put her clothes in.

He followed her over. "I think you're giving me reason to be, don't you?"

"Don't worry," she said, "I'm not following you." But he didn't hear the words because now his eyes were glued to the book by Nabokov she had under her arm. In sheer panic, he fled.

"Mr. Lacayo?"

"Yes?" He sounded suspicious.

"This is Jill. I have your clothes—dried, folded and ready to go. I don't do ironing." She was trying her best not to laugh, but it wasn't easy.

"Oh, my God!"

"If you'd like to pick them up, my address is—"

"What are you trying to do to me?"

Why was he screaming? "I was just trying to be helpful."

"I don't *need* your help. The last thing in the world I want is your help. What is the matter with you, young lady? Do you miss your father? Are you out to ruin my career? Have you taken complete leave of your senses?"

"Listen, Mr. Lacayo—"

"Don't interrupt when I'm speaking! I am a teacher, you are a student, and there's nothing in the world that can change that fact. Do I make myself clear?"

"First of all—"

"I told you not to interrupt me. I do not want you showing up at my house. I do not want you following me to the laundromat. I do not want you hassling me in class. In short, will you *please lay off*?"

"I really think you're behaving childishly," she said, starting to get annoyed. He was coming off fatherly, which she really resented.

"I'm behaving childishly?"

"Yes."

"*I'm* behaving childishly?"

"You're repeating yourself, Mr. Lacayo," she said, and in return had the phone slammed down in her ear. That made two times in two days. She was beginning to think she'd forgotten the art of telephone conversation.

"SO HOW'D IT GO?" asked Trader, coming in the door with a satisfied smile on his face.

"How did what go?"

"You and Sally."

Doug shrugged. "Look, she wasn't my type."

"Am I hearing you right?"

"You're the one who goes for petite brunettes, Trader. I'm more into—"

"High school students?"

"That isn't what I was going to say. I just didn't care for Sally, that's all. So, are you seeing Donna again?"

"*Again?*"

"Yeah, you know, like another time?"

"What for?"

"I don't know, maybe to get to know her."

"I got to know her."

"You're an animal, Woleski, you know it? You *use* women."

"It was mutual. Listen, we're equal these days, haven't you heard?"

"I'm just talking about decent human behavior."

"Well, let me tell you something about decent human behavior, Lacayo. You listening?"

"You're aggravating me, Woleski."

"Donna got what she wanted last night. I left her happy. Can you say the same for Sally?"

"I gave her a ride home like you asked."

"Right. You disappointed her. You did not come through. Are you telling me that's decent human behavior?"

"You make it sound logical, Trader, but there's something wrong in your reasoning."

"There's nothing wrong in my reasoning. I treated Donna as an equal. You treated Sally like you thought you were too good for her."

"It's not a question of being too good for her."

"You're a snob, Lacayo."

"She didn't appeal to me, okay? Sexual attraction is pretty hard to fake when you get a woman into bed."

"How would *you* know?"

"You act like I'm celibate or something."

"All I can say, Dougie, is that if it weren't for me, this place would resemble a monastery."

"Look, I've had a bad enough day, Woleski, I don't need you crawling up my back."

"Did you do the laundry?"

"I want to talk to you about that."

"What's to talk about? It's your week." Trader walked into his room and came right back out. "Where'd you put my clothes?"

"You're not going to believe this, Woleski."

"Try me."

Doug sighed. "I left them at the laundromat."

"Big deal, so go back and get them. I'll go with you. We'll stop and get something to eat."

"You don't understand."

"I'm trying to. Why don't you make yourself clear?"

Doug tried to think of a good way to word it, but could only come up with, "Jill took them home with her."

"Excuse me?"

"I said, Jill—"

"I *heard* what you said."

"She's the one—"

"I *know* who she is."

"She happened to be there—"

"Are you completely deranged, Lacayo, meeting one of your students at the laundromat?"

"Take it easy, Trader—"

"How do you expect me to take it easy?"

"If you'd just let me explain what—"

Trader held up his hand for silence. "I'm getting the picture, Lacayo, believe me. I just wish I'd gotten the picture a little sooner. Tell me, were you secretly dating ten-year-olds in college?"

"I'm sorry. I saw her there and I panicked."

"Wait a minute, wait a minute. You saw her where?"

"At the laundromat."

"And the sight of her was enough to make you panic?"

"You're not going to believe this."

"Maybe not, but we'll never know unless you tell me."

"She had this book with her—"

"Oh, right. A book."

"...*Lolita*."

"Oh, God."

"Exactly."

"You better not be putting me on."

"It was innocent, Woleski, I swear. My laundry was almost done by the time she came in. I don't know, I just lost control when I saw the book."

"Just tell me this, Lacayo. What the hell am I supposed to wear to work tomorrow?"

JILL WALKED INTO civics on Monday morning wearing Mr. Lacayo's blue-and-white-striped shirt with her new denim skirt. A button was missing off one of the cuffs, but she would've rolled up the sleeves anyway. The teacher wasn't there to see her entrance, but she couldn't wait to see his expression when he caught sight of his shirt. Greg smiled at her. Barry glanced in her direction and then pointedly looked away. Peter winked at her. By the time she made her way to the back row, Alan and his two friends were laughing openly.

"I hear you've got the next best thing to a hot line," said Alan.

"What's that supposed to mean?"

"I hear you had the boys' phones ringing off the hooks this weekend."

"I decided to go into action," said Jill.

"And the date with Peter Rabbit? How'd that go?"

"Where do you get your news, Alan, from informants?"

"Half the school saw you out with him."

"The movie was pretty good," she said.

"I wasn't asking for a movie review."

"What do you want to know?"

"Peter has a reputation for roving hands."

"And well earned," said Jill. "I would think the daughter of missionaries would get a little more respect."

Alan chuckled with enjoyment. "Somehow, it's Peter I'm feeling sorry for."

Lacayo walked in, took roll, and when he got to Jill's name and looked back at her, he visibly paled. Either he recognized his shirt, or the encounter in the laundromat had proved traumatic. If he weren't so cute, she'd begin to lose interest in him. Acting scared to death of her like that wasn't attractive, nor was the way he had lectured her on the phone as if he was the very worst kind of school principal. Didn't the man have a sense of humor?

TUESDAY MEANT PIZZA at Mario's, and Trader came back to the table carrying an extra-large with everything on it.

"By the way," he said, "I saw Lolita in the hall this morning and, if I'm not mistaken, she was wearing one of my shirts. The green Izod my mother sent me for Christmas. I like that shirt."

"It looked good on her," said Doug.

"I want my clothes back, Lacayo."

"What do you expect me to do, Woleski, rip it off her back?"

Trader dropped the piece of pizza he was holding. "Don't even joke around like that."

"She wore one of mine yesterday, right in front of the whole class. They must have seen me in that shirt a couple dozen times."

"I kind of admire her sense of humor."

"She's enjoying it, too. I personally fail to see the humor."

"In the meantime, though, I have nothing to wear."

Doug sighed. "I'll buy you a shirt, okay?"

"You'll buy me several."

"We'll drive down to Sears tonight."

"Sears? You expect me to wear a shirt from Sears?"

"It's either that or Goodwill, Woleski—take your pick."

"Let's just hope she isn't wearing our jockeys."

A FRONT-PAGE STORY on Wednesday morning played right into Jill's hands. The son of a famous movie star committed suicide in a bizarre fashion, announcing his intentions to the control tower before nose diving into the surf in Santa Monica near the movie star's house.

When Lacayo asked the class if they had read anything of interest in the papers that morning, only Jill raised her hand. She could see he was hesitant to call on her, but since half the class saw her raised hand he finally nodded to her.

"Bolo Murphy's son killed himself," she said.

The class picked up a little at that. Bolo Murphy was the star of several science fiction movies particularly popular with kids.

Lacayo glossed over the main points of the story, obviously not thinking it of value in current events. When he tried to move on to other news, Jill raised her hand again.

"Yes, Jill?" His eyes were studiously avoiding his brown checked shirt she was wearing that day with her jeans.

"I wondered if you had any ideas why kids kill themselves."

"I believe he was twenty-one," said Doug.

"I know, but that isn't very old and he seemed to have everything."

"Teen suicide? Is that what you want to address here?"

The class went preternaturally silent and Jill began to grow uncomfortable. Only a desire to find out what happened to Susan made her say, "Yes. I wonder about it sometimes."

She looked around, but most of the students were staring down at their desks. She wasn't the only one feeling uncomfortable.

Lacayo pushed his hands through his hair and audibly sighed. He got up behind his desk and came around the front to perch on the edge of the desk. He looked serious. "I know we haven't talked about the fact that one of your former classmates killed herself," he said, "but I think maybe it's about time we did." He looked straight at Jill. "You wouldn't know about it; it happened before you came here, but she was in this civics class."

"Are you talking about that girl who drowned herself?" asked someone seated in the front. The class visibly squirmed at the words.

"Yes, I am," said Lacayo. "I'm talking about Susan Peters. And we probably should have talked about it when it happened. So tell me, why do kids kill themselves? Do any of you have any ideas?"

"Maybe she was having trouble at home," said one of the boys, and a few of the others nodded.

"Maybe," said Lacayo. "Would you consider suicide if you were having trouble at home?"

The silence was grim.

"What about school? Do the pressures here ever get to you?"

"Yeah, too much homework," one of the jocks yelled out, but the usual laughter wasn't forthcoming.

He finally got a discussion going, albeit a reluctant one. Jill found, however, that it was too painful to listen to and she finally had to tune it out. She wasn't hearing any clues about what happened to her sister, as she had hoped. Instead she was hearing things she didn't want to hear: young people they had heard of who had overdosed on drugs, stories they had heard about abused children, modern equivalents of Romeo and Juliet. None were related as firsthand experiences; all were something they had "heard about." She was sorry she had instigated the discussion and felt relieved when Lacayo finally dropped it and turned to more political news.

Jill felt traumatized by it for the rest of the day, and the next day she called the school and said she was sick, then made arrangements to meet her parents in Miami for lunch.

"DARLING, you look tired," said her mother.

"It's all the homework," said Jill. "I don't remember ever studying this hard in high school."

"But why study?" asked her dad. "It's not as though you're really going to graduate."

"You know me—once an A student, always an A student."

"There's a word for that," said her mother.

"I know, I know," said Jill.

They talked a little about Susan, how Jill wasn't getting anywhere with her investigation, but how she was also convinced it hadn't been suicide. Then, because she'd managed to make them all morose, she told them about her encounters with Mr. Lacayo at his home and also at the laundromat, and finally had her father laughing and her mother smiling.

"Poor man," said her dad. "He'll probably give up teaching after this."

"Really, Jill, you could get him in trouble," said her mother.

"I know it makes me sound like a brat, but the thing is, I'm really interested in him. He's funny and intelligent and he's a good teacher."

"Do you meet any men over in Africa?" asked her mother.

"Oh, sure," said Jill, "but so far no one who interests me."

"We're hoping—" said her father, breaking off in mid-sentence.

"I know, you're hoping I'll stay here," said Jill.

"It would be lovely having you close," said her mother.

"I can't," said Jill, "I have to go back. There's too much to do over there and not enough people to do it. Anyway, this is retirement land down here. It's hard to take Florida seriously."

"At least you'll spend the summer with us, won't you?" asked her mother.

"Yes. I'll spend the summer." And if she played her cards right, she might be able to spend the summer with Mr. Lacayo, too. Poor man, he'd probably be even more traumatized if he knew the plans she had for him.

ON FRIDAY MARLA came up to Jill in the P.E. locker room. Jill was sure it was going to be another tennis challenge, but instead Marla said, "I'm having a party Saturday night, Jill, if you want to come."

Jill knew that as the new girl she was supposed to be overjoyed at the invitation, but she couldn't take high school politicking seriously. "You mean you're actually inviting me to a party, Marla?"

For a moment Marla looked as though she was about to rescind the invitation, then she forged ahead anyway. "I hear you and Alan are going together and—"

"I'm not going with Alan," said Jill. "We're just friends."

Marla, who had probably not been given a hard time in years, looked about to retreat again.

"But thanks anyway," said Jill.

Marla sighed. "I invited Alan and he said he'd come if you were coming."

Jill pictured herself home alone on Saturday night in front of the TV set. She didn't know which was worse. "Well, give me your address," she said. "Maybe I'll come."

"Just dress casual," said Marla, running her eyes over Jill's clothes, which consisted of her usual jeans and another of Lacayo's shirts.

"I always dress casual," said Jill.

"I've noticed."

IT WAS LIKE no high school party Jill had ever been to. It was very much like some of the college parties she had attended, though, so she wasn't in the least shocked. The beer was plentiful, the lights were low, the music was loud, and any evidence of Marla's parents was nonexistent. Sliding glass doors were open onto a patio with a swimming pool beyond, and unless her eyes were suddenly going bad, Jill thought she saw some skinny-dipping going on.

She had worn shorts and a T-shirt, and for once she was dressed like everyone else. She grabbed herself a beer and headed outdoors where some kids were dancing. She saw Alan and David and Mark standing by themselves and walked over to them.

"I'm here because of you," she said to Alan, her voice accusing.

"I just wanted to shake up Marla," said Alan. "She hated having to put her seal of approval on you."

"I hated letting her."

"I just thought you ought to see a generic Palm Cove High School party," Alan said. "Just consider it anthropological research."

"Watching the natives?"

He smiled. "Something like that. Do you dance?"

"Not if I can help it."

"Do you swim?"

Jill glanced at the pool. "I didn't bring a suit."

"Neither did they."

"So I see."

"You don't looked shocked, Jill. I would think a well-brought-up daughter of missionaries would be blushing about now."

"Really, Alan, and I would've thought an intelligent boy like you would've read *National Geographic*. Or at least looked at the pictures."

Alan burst out laughing. "You see what I mean?" he said to his friends. "I told you, she's different."

Marla stopped by to say, "Why don't you guys dance?"

They ignored her, and as she headed off in a huff, David said to Alan, "Not too obvious or anything."

"She's hot for you, man," said Mark.

"Why don't you give her a break and dance with her?" asked Jill.

"I dated Marla in the seventh grade," said Alan, "and she was just as boring then. What you've got to understand is we've known these girls all our lives."

Mark grinned at her. "We're waiting for college to meet some new ones."

Jill saw Peter heading her way, weaving through the dancers with a big smile on his face. She swore under her breath.

"What's the matter?" Alan asked her, but by that time Peter was right there.

"Want to dance?" he asked Jill.

"Not to this music," she said. "I don't trust you in a slow dance."

"Hey, there's people all around," said Peter.

Jill took a look at the dancers. Their bodies were pressed together so tightly that if there weren't any music, it would bear no resemblance to dancing.

"No, thanks," she reiterated.

"Go ask Marla," suggested Alan. "She's looking for someone to dance with."

When the music changed to another slow tune and Alan held his hand out to her, she found herself moving into his arms and putting her own around his neck. He had such self-confidence, was in so much control when he danced, that she had to keep reminding herself he was only a kid. He didn't act like one, though, and he sure didn't dance like one. If she were really seventeen she'd be in danger of falling for his charm.

"Act like you're enjoying it," Alan whispered in her ear, and she saw that Marla was watching them with barely an attempt at hiding her jealousy.

"Why are you playing games with Marla?" she asked him.

"Because she thinks she's hot stuff, and she needs to be taken down a peg."

"That's beneath your intelligence, Alan."

She felt his lips on her neck as he murmured, "She can't understand how the daughter of missionaries could possibly be competition. She's trying to figure out what I see in you."

"Thanks a lot."

"Hey, you're worth ten of her. She doesn't understand that a guy might want a little more than perfectly placed sun streaks and a miniskirt up to her crotch."

"You're being nasty."

"I enjoy a little mental stimulation, but all she's offering is a good time in the backseat of a car."

"I'm not offering anything, Alan."

"I know."

"I mean it. No games."

He moved his head around so that they were face to face. When he leaned in to kiss her, he took her by surprise, and not wanting to cause a scene, she let him kiss her. What was most astonishing was how really proficient he was.

He broke away. "Hey, act like you're enjoying it; we have an audience."

The trouble was, she was enjoying it. There was something charismatic about him that wasn't wasted on her. Plus, she missed being in a man's arms and Lacayo was beginning to seem out of reach. *He's seventeen, for God's sake,* she admonished herself. But he didn't feel seventeen and he didn't sound seventeen, and if the music hadn't changed over to something fast she wasn't sure she would have walked away from him.

"I'm cutting out," said Jill, when they had formed their little group again.

"So soon?" asked Alan.

"This is a waste of time."

"That it is," he said. "You want to go get something to eat with us?" His eyes held hers for a moment and she was the first to look away.

"Not tonight," she said.

Alan shrugged. "We'll follow you, see that you get home all right."

"Marla's going to be crushed," said Jill.

"I know. Isn't it beautiful?"

DOUG SAT IN FRONT of the television set and wondered what his problem was. He was twenty-nine, he was single, up until now he had always considered his sexual appetite to be healthy, but instead of going out with Trader and having a good time, he was sitting in a recliner like an old man, watching the tube. He was beginning, in fact, to resemble his father.

Hell, even his students probably had a better sex life than he did.

You're in deep trouble, Lacayo, he told himself. *You've become fixated on an underage student who stole your clothes and makes a fool out of you in class.*

He should've stayed in Chicago.

He felt the walls closing in on him. Hell, he felt the world closing in on him. He was very close to crossing over the line from normal behavior to aberrant behavior. He was very close to committing a crime. After twenty-nine years of clean living, how had he come to be a potential child molester?

Not that she was a child. None of the senior girls seemed like children, and in a matter of a few months he could even legally date them. But it had never happened to him before. Even when he was younger, closer in age to his students, he'd never felt any attraction toward them. Those kinds of thoughts hadn't even entered his mind, and on the rare occasions when he heard of a high school teacher dating one of the students, it had always disgusted him.

Well, welcome to the club. He was now one of those abhorrent men who preyed on young girls. He had to actually fight off the urge to walk into the school office and look up her address. He was a sicko, and he didn't foresee getting any better in the near future.

It wasn't really his fault, of course. *He* hadn't started it. She'd been coming on to him since her first day in class. Girls like that shouldn't be allowed in high schools. In his day, high school girls who came on to teachers were considered tramps.

Well, let's be reasonable, Lacayo, she isn't really a tramp. She's just an intelligent girl who's almost a woman and she's probably just having a good time with you.

Trader was right, wearing the shirts showed a good sense of humor. And he hadn't exactly been acting like an adult when he had bolted out of the laundromat, leaving the clothes behind. It was just that that was the kind of effect she had on him. Or maybe it was fear of what he might do.

Lolita? That had to be a signal. There was nothing subtle about carrying that particular book and just happening to run into him. She had probably planned it every step of the way and laughed herself silly at his reaction.

What the hell was she up to? If she was as intelligent as she seemed, why would she go to a male teacher's house? Were missionaries' daughters that naive? Is that how things were done in Ethiopia? Well, maybe they were. Maybe he had been totally inhospitable. Maybe he was seeing motives that were really innocent, but since *he* wasn't feeling innocent, he was attributing them to her.

He'd always thought he could tell when an attraction was mutual. He couldn't remember ever being wrong about that. He was convinced she was just as attracted to him, but that didn't necessarily mean that she knew what she was doing. She was only seventeen, for God's sake. Yeah, and in lots of places girls were already married at seventeen.

The one lesson he was learning out of all of it was that he damn well had to get out of teaching. He wished he could get out of it before Monday, but he'd somehow muddle through the rest of the school year, trying to stay out of her way, trying to discourage her, and when summer came, he'd get the hell out of Florida.

But in the meantime, it was a dilemma.

Chapter Seven

He called me up. I couldn't believe it! I know Mom
could hear me talking and that made me nervous.
We're going to meet tomorrow after school. I'm so
excited I know I'll never be able to sleep tonight. I
don't think he'd want to meet me if he didn't feel
the same way I do. At least that's what I'm hoping.

"SPRING FLING," announced the posters around
school. Everywhere Jill turned she heard girls asking
girls, "Are you going to the dance?" In the halls she
heard boys asking boys, "Who're you taking to the
dance?" Even Phaedra, with no date in sight, couldn't
stop talking about it. It was the special dance of the
year, put on in the ballroom of a grand old hotel on the
beach, and Jill could've sworn Haile Selassie had come
back from the dead and was giving a royal ball the way
everyone was carrying on.

What made her finally prick up her ears was Mr. Lacayo saying in class, "How many of you are going to the
dance?"

About two-thirds of the hands went up.

"What's the matter with the rest of you dead-beats?" he admonished them. "Where's your school spirit?"

Jill heard Alan mutter, "What school spirit?"

"Listen," said Lacayo, "if I have to show up in a monkey suit to chaperone you guys, the least you could do is keep me company."

Jill's eyes shifted to Lacayo's, but he wasn't looking at her. She wondered if that had been a thinly veiled invitation. More likely he was breathing a deep sigh of relief at the news that she wasn't going.

"Want to go to the dance?" said the note Alan passed to her.

"Are you asking me to the dance, Alan?" she wrote back.

"I just thought you might think it was a big deal to go."

"Do you have to have a date to go?"

She heard him chuckle before writing back, "It's not required, but I've never heard of a girl showing up alone."

"I might try it."

He gave her a look before scribbling, "I always said you were different."

The class was almost out of control, talking among themselves about the dance, so that when Lacayo broached the subject of the new arms treaty, Jill had an idea she was the only one who even heard him. She didn't bite. It wasn't the kind of subject that called for arguing.

She saw Lacayo finally give up, sit back down at his desk and wait for the bell.

JILL LET PHAEDRA go on and on about the dance, and when she finally stopped talking long enough to start on her lunch, Jill said, "Let's go."

"I'm not finished yet."

"To the dance, Phaedra. Let's go stag."

Phaedra's mouth dropped open, revealing unappetizing bits of hotdog and mustard. "You can't do that."

"It's not against the law," said Jill.

"Everyone would laugh at us."

"So what?"

"But it's a *dance*. What's the point of going to a dance if no one will dance with you? Not that no one would dance with you, but I'd just be standing around looking stupid."

"Come on, they have mostly rock music, don't they?"

"Yeah."

"So we'll dance together. Just not the slow dances."

"I'd die of embarrassment."

"Have you ever been to a school dance, Phaedra?"

"Not since junior high, and then everyone went."

"Didn't the girls dance together?"

"Sure, but we were just kids then."

"I'm sure they still do," said Jill, although she wasn't sure at all.

"Forget it, I'm sorry I mentioned the dance."

"I'm going," said Jill, "and if you want to go with me, that's fine. If you don't, I'm going anyway."

"You wouldn't have the nerve. Well, I guess you would."

"What do they wear?"

"It's formal."

"Really formal? You mean like long dresses?"

"I've seen a lot of short formals in the stores, but I think most of the girls are wearing long."

"We'll go shopping after school. Will your mom buy you a formal?"

"Sure, will yours?"

"I've got enough money for one. How about letting me pick yours out?"

"You're going to turn me into Cinderella, right?"

"You want to give it a try?"

Phaedra grimaced. "Listen, if I thought it was possible, I would've tried it myself."

"I think it's possible."

"Maybe with a magic wand."

THE DRESS was purple and gauzy and outrageous. It plunged in the front to reveal Phaedra's ample decolletage, folded in floating wings over her upper arms and draped in layers of uneven lengths to her ankles. Rather than looking like a fat girl squeezed into too small clothes, she looked lusty and sexy and not a little bizarre.

"It's definitely you," said Jill.

Phaedra was turning around in front of the mirror admiring herself. "It's not bad," she said. "I think I look older."

"You definitely look older."

"Maybe I could do something with my hair."

"Something fantastic," said Jill, "like maybe about a hundred little braids with purple ribbon floating out the ends of them."

"You going to do 'em?"

"Sure. And makeup. Lots of purple eyeshadow and kohl around your eyes."

"What's kohl?"

"It's like eyeliner."

"I still don't think anyone will dance with me, but at least I'll like the way I look. What about you? You getting the black one?"

"I don't know."

"You looked great in it. Sophisticated. Anyone would think you were at least twenty."

Or thirty, which was exactly what she was worried about. The black did suit her, but she thought she'd better try for a more youthful look.

Although it might be fun to show up looking sexy in black and ask Lacayo to dance. If he ran away from her in shorts in the laundromat, he'd probably fall through the floor if he saw her in the slinky black number.

DOUG SNAPPED ON the bow tie. "How late is this thing going to last?"

"This is the biggie. The band'll probably play until two in the morning."

"I feel ridiculous in this tux."

"The school's paying for it."

"I wasn't complaining about the cost, Woleski."

"You look like a prince."

"Yeah, right, as long as my sweat socks don't show."

"All we've got to do is stand around, sneak out to the bar for an occasional drink, and make sure the students aren't sneaking out more often than we are. The main thing is to prevent the kids from driving while intoxicated."

"Why don't they just not serve booze?"

"They don't, but the hotel is in business to make money, and liquor's where the money is."

"We don't have to dance, do we?"

"It wouldn't kill you to ask some of the female chaperones to dance, Lacayo."

"I don't know."

"Just lay off the students."

"What're you talking about?"

"They're going to ask you to dance."

"What, is that against the law or something?"

"Just not Jill, okay?"

"You think I'm nuts?"

"As a matter of fact—"

"Give me a break, Woleski! I'm not going near her."

"Well, she'll probably ask you to dance, and all I'm saying is—"

"No way. She won't ask me to dance."

"I don't think I'm out of the ballpark on this. She did accost you in the laundromat, she did show up at our house, and she does wear your clothes."

"*Our* clothes."

"Whatever."

"She's been ignoring me lately. I mean other than the clothes."

"Reverse psychology."

"Baloney."

"Yeah, you said she's smart, didn't you? Well, going after you didn't work, so now she's trying to make you go after her."

"Fat chance."

"You're not fooling me, you know."

"Get serious, Woleski."

"If she were eighteen and you were all alone with her, are you telling me you'd walk away?"

"Pure supposition."

"That's what I meant it to be."

"Well, it doesn't matter because she's not going to the dance."

"How do you know?"

"I asked the class who was going, and she didn't raise her hand."

"So that's why you don't want to go."

"Will you knock it off? She's just a kid, Woleski, and I don't go for kids!"

"Of course not. Particularly since it might land you in jail."

"QUIT SLUMPING," Jill ordered Phaedra, who as soon as they entered had gone into her fat-girl walk.

"I can't help it."

"You look terrific," Jill told her, "I want you to try flaunting it. If you believe you're something, the other kids will start believing it, too."

Phaedra threw her shoulders back and lifted her chin. Her face wore a look of uncertainty, though. "My natural inclination is to hide under a sheet, you know."

"Not tonight."

"I'll try."

"You'll succeed! And quit looking at the boys. Ignore them. Boys can't stand to be ignored."

Jill steered her around the dance floor to the table holding an assortment of soft drinks, which were mostly being ignored by the students.

"You don't ignore them," groused Phaedra. "You're always flirting with them."

"Yes, but it's okay to flirt if you're not interested. But if you flirt when you're interested, it makes you look desperate."

"I am desperate," said Phaedra.

"Just listen to me, okay? Just for tonight."

"Okay, fairy godmother."

Jill grabbed two Cokes and handed one to Phaedra. "I'll have someone get us something stronger later."

"I don't drink," said Phaedra.

"You need something to relax you."

"Doesn't Mr. Lacayo look handsome in a tux?"

Jill froze. *"Where?"*

"Right—"

"Don't point."

"All right," said Phaedra. "I don't know why you keep yelling at me."

Jill sneaked a glance at Lacayo. He looked good, but she thought she liked him better in his regular clothes. He looked as uncomfortable as she was feeling in high heels.

"You really did it," said Alan, and she turned to see him, Mark and David trailing in his wake.

"I told you I was going to."

"I know. I told the guys we had to come see this. David bet me five bucks you wouldn't show."

"Sorry, David," she said to him.

David grinned. "It was worth it."

"You want to dance?" Alan asked her.

Jill shook her head. "I'm dancing with Phaedra."

Alan turned to look around and did a double-take when he saw Phaedra. "Lookin' good," he said to her, then some signal passed between Alan and Mark and Mark asked Phaedra to dance.

Alan held his hand out to Jill and she took it.

SHE WAS WEARING a short, silky black dress that clung to her thighs and plunged down the back. She was all slim limbs and smooth back and she made all the other girls there look overdressed and silly.

Doug nudged Trader. "Did you see her?"

"See who?"

Doug shook his head.

"Yeah, I saw her. She sure isn't wearing our clothes tonight."

"Not so loud, Woleski."

"Relax."

"How could she even wear underwear under that?"

Doug watched as Trader's eyes scanned Jill on the dance floor. "I see what you mean. She's a hot little number, isn't she?"

"You're talking about a child, Woleski."

"Hey, you're the one who noticed her. Anyway, she doesn't look like much of a child out there. It's amazing what a change of clothes will do, isn't it?"

"WILL YOU DO ME a favor, Alan?"

"Don't worry, I'll dance with Phaedra."

Jill looked over his shoulder and saw that Phaedra was now dancing with David. "How come your friends are dancing with her?"

"Why shouldn't they?"

"No reason. It's just that you usually ignore her."

"She's usually ignorable."

"She looks good, doesn't she?"

"Not good, but interesting. We decided to shake things up here tonight, and dancing with Phaedra is as good a way as any. We'll make her look like the most popular girl at the dance."

"And then forget about her on Monday."

"So she'll have a night to remember. What's so bad about that?"

IT WAS BAD ENOUGH watching Jill switch from a fast dance with Singer to a slow one. It was worse when he saw the two of them slip out to the bar. He supposed he should head for the bar himself and police their action, but something held him back.

First he had been afraid she'd ask him to dance. Now he was feeling ignored because she hadn't. For the coach to be feeling jealous of his star pitcher was embarrassing. It was beneath him. It lacked any kind of dignity at all. But he could see himself walking into the bar, grabbing him by the throat and choking him.

So much for being an adult.

JILL BOUGHT TWO DRINKS in the bar and met Phaedra in the ladies' room. She handed one to the girl and said, "Drink up. It'll make you relax."

"I didn't know missionaries drank," said Phaedra.

"Some of them do."

Phaedra took a sip and made a face. "It tastes awful."

"Of course it does, but wait until you feel the effect."

Jill ran some cold water over a paper towel and patted off her face. The only makeup she had on was some mascara and a little eye shadow, but her cheeks were flushed pink from the exercise. "Are you having fun?"

"What did you do, pay those guys to dance with me?"

"Don't be silly."

"How come boys are dancing with me?"

"Well, no one's forcing them to, so they must want to."

"All the girls with dates are looking at us as though they wished we'd drop dead."

"Maybe we'll start a new trend, going to dances alone."

Phaedra finished off her drink and smiled. "I feel warm all over."

"Do the teachers ever dance with the students?"

"You're asking me? I've never been to one of these dances."

"In Africa it would've been okay."

"I wouldn't mind asking Mr. Lacayo to dance," said Phaedra. "I'd probably just embarrass him, though."

"Why don't you try it?" asked Jill, thinking that if Phaedra asked him first, it wouldn't look so strange if she asked him.

"I wouldn't have the nerve."

"What you need is another drink."

"HOW MANY MORE hours of this do we have?" asked Annie Lopez.

"Too many," said Doug, wondering why he had asked her to dance. Maybe it was because Jill never seemed to be without a partner and he was tired of standing on the sidelines. And because Annie was nice, and also safely married with two kids.

"At least we'll get to miss the senior prom."

He maneuvered Annie over next to where Jill was dancing with a boy he didn't know. When she saw him over the boy's shoulder, she smiled and said, "Hello, Mr. Lacayo."

"Hello, Jill," he mumbled, wishing she didn't sound as if she was having such a good time.

"Nice girl," said Annie.

"Is Jill in your class?"

"Yes, but I don't know why. She speaks Spanish as fluently as I do."

"Spanish? I thought she was living in Africa."

"Her parents were in Central America before that. She's got an ear for languages. She also speaks French and several of the African dialects."

"She's up on current events, too," said Doug.

"I would imagine so."

"Yeah."

"Is it just me, or does she seem older to you?"

"Well, that black dress—"

"I don't mean just the dress. It's the way she speaks to me, the way she is around the other students. She's certainly the most self-possessed senior I've ever had."

"She's probably been with adults a lot."

"What's this dance step you're doing, Doug?"

"I'm not sure. Are you having trouble following it?"

"I've just never done it before."

"Want to go to the bar and get a drink?"

Annie dropped her arms and smiled. "I thought you'd never ask."

"I'M GOING TO ASK Mr. Lacayo to dance," said Jill, once more dancing with Alan. She had danced with about a dozen other boys, but he was the only one she felt comfortable with. He wasn't trying to get too close or put any moves on her tonight; he was just being a buddy.

"You might as well," said Alan. "He probably hasn't had a good argument all night."

"Shake him up a little."

"Go for it," said Alan. "He's just standing over there by himself looking morose."

Jill took a look. "Yeah, he does look morose. I think it's my duty to cheer him up."

"Consider it school spirit."

"But I think I'll wait for a slow one."

"Uh-oh!"

"Just out of consideration for his age, Alan. Have you seen him try to dance fast?"

"He's not too graceful for an athlete."

"No, he isn't." And she had a feeling he'd lose any grace he had when she approached him. She'd never felt such power of intimidation over a person before and she rather relished it.

HE SAW A SWIRLING dark shadow out of the corner of his eye, and then Jill was in front of him, a phony-looking smile of singular innocence on her face.

"Will you dance with me, Mr. Lacayo?" Her voice was sweet enough to attract flies.

"Well, uh..."

"It's a slow one."

"Yeah, but..."

"Come on, you've got to enjoy yourself."

He gave her a dubious look. "Yeah, all right, Jill." He moved out to the dance floor with her and held out his arms. She moved into them a little too quickly and he could feel himself starting to sweat.

He kept a distance of a couple of inches between them, but still her nose was almost up against his mouth. He glanced around the room to see if anyone was watching them and saw Trader, eyes popping out of his head, looking at him in alarm. Doug moved back another inch.

"Oh, Mr. Lacayo, isn't this fun?" asked Jill, a perky tone to her voice he had never heard before. It was like a bad imitation of a teenager.

"Well, uh...."

"I've never been to a high school dance before."

"No dances where you were?"

She shook her head and her soft hair brushed against his lips. It smelled clean with the faint hint of almonds. He turned his head away from her a little and tried to breath in some fresh air.

"You seem to be doing all right," said Doug, thinking that it was better to keep the talking going than to risk a long silence with her in his arms.

"You mean my dancing?"

"No, your dancing's fine. I mean the boys all seem to like you."

"Yes, and I was afraid no one would dance with me because I didn't have a date."

"You came alone?"

"I came with another girl."

"I thought you were with Singer."

"Alan doesn't date."

Another couple brushed up against them and Jill moved in closer to him. Doug enjoyed the body contact for a moment before putting space between them again. "So how are you enjoying Palm Cove?"

"It seems superficial."

"Well, yeah..." And wasn't he the striking conversationalist tonight? He was tripping over his tongue at about the same rate he was tripping over his feet.

She moved her hand from his shoulder and he could feel it come to rest on the back of his neck. His palm started to sweat and he was sure she could notice it.

"You going to college next year?" he asked her.

"I'm planning to."

"Where're you going?"

"I was thinking of California."

"Oh, well, if you find this place superficial—"

"Berkeley."

"You should fit right in."

"Because I like to argue?"

"You've got a good mind."

"Thank you, Mr. Lacayo. Sometimes I get the feeling you wish I'd shut up in class."

"I enjoy our arguments," said Doug.

She leaned her head back and looked into his eyes. She had a look in her eyes he had never seen before, and he attributed it to the fact she was wearing eye makeup. "I enjoy them, too," she said, and her voice went from teenage to something of a caress.

Doug put a little more distance between them. "What are you going to major in in college?" he asked, wondering when this particular song was ever going to end.

"Biology."

"Why biology?"

"I like it. I'd like to do research."

"Well, I'm sure you'll do fine at it."

She chuckled.

"What's so funny?"

"I'm making you nervous, aren't I?"

"No, not at all. I'm just not much of a dancer; anyone makes me nervous."

"I'm sorry about coming to your house like that."

"Forget it!"

"No, I really want to apologize."

"No need," said Doug, hoping this wasn't going to get personal and not knowing how to head it off if it was.

"I just had to talk to you and you weren't in the phone book."

"No problem."

"I didn't realize you'd be so shocked. In Africa we go over to the teachers' houses all the time. It's much more informal."

"I can see where it might be."

"Sometimes we even dated the teachers. They weren't much older than we were."

"That's not done here," said Doug. "That's against the rules. We're not supposed to socialize with the students at all."

"That's too bad," she said, sounding like a child once again. But then she moved in against him and she didn't feel like a child at all. He could tell by the feel that she wasn't wearing a bra and it flustered him. Just as he was about to push her away, she moved back of her own accord.

"Do you have any brothers and sisters?"

"No."

"You must be homesick."

"A little. When I dream at night it's always about Africa."

He breathed a sigh of relief. For a moment there he thought she was going to say she dreamed about him, which wouldn't be acceptable at all. Forget that twice he had dreamed about her.

"Ms. Lopez says you lived in Central America."

"Yes, before Africa."

"I'm envious. I've never been out of the States except to Canada a couple of times."

"I haven't been in the States much."

Doug could tell by the music that the song was about to end, and he began to breathe easier. So when she moved her mouth to his ear to whisper, he was taken completely by surprise.

"Can I tell you a secret?" she whispered.

"Sure, Jill," he said, trying to sound avuncular.

"I sleep in your underwear."

"WHAT'D YOU SAY to Lacayo?" asked Alan. "He looks like you hit him over the head with a baseball bat."

"We were just having a political argument," said Jill, trying not to laugh as she saw Lacayo huddled with Mr. Woleski across the room.

"You must've won."

"I guess you could say that."

"YOU CAN'T WALK OUT like this. You're a chaperone, for God's sake," Trader reminded him.

"She's got me running scared, Woleski."

"Come on, we'll go into the bar and I'll buy you a drink."

Doug let himself be led to the bar, but a drink wasn't going to help. Sure, it might temporarily numb him, but it wasn't going to change the situation.

"Tell me again what she said."

"I told you," said Doug, lowering his voice and looking around to see if anyone was listening. "She said she slept in my underwear."

"Of course it could be mine," said Trader. "It's not as though we have name tags in it."

"That's not the point! The point is, was that an extremely provocative remark or am I imagining things?"

"Oh, yeah, it was provocative all right. Talk about Lolita."

"Don't even say that."

"I think it's time for you to take certain steps, Doug."

"Yeah, like as many steps as it'll take to get me out of here."

"What's she going to do, attack you on the dance floor? Just don't dance with her if she asks you again. I don't like to say I told you so, but you shouldn't have danced with her in the first place."

"But she wasn't acting like that then. She was acting like a regular teenager."

"You should've known from past experience that that wouldn't last."

"You want to hear the worst part? I wanted to dance with her."

"Hell, I know that."

"What am I going to do?"

"As I said, you've got to take certain steps. I think we ought to go to the principal on Monday."

"And try to explain how one of my students is sleeping in my jockey shorts?"

"Did she specifically say 'jockey shorts'? Maybe she's just sleeping in one of our T-shirts."

"Does it really matter?"

"I guess not," said Trader. "But John's a good guy, I think he'd listen to you."

"Oh, yeah, he's really going to believe some innocent daughter of missionaries is coming on to me."

"The thing is, you've got me as a witness. I was there when she came by the house."

"You'd testify for me?"

"We're not going to court, Doug. Sure I'll back you up with John. Kids have come on to teachers before; this is nothing new."

"And teachers have come on to kids."

"Yeah, but nothing's happened yet so I don't see why he wouldn't believe you."

"Monday, huh?"

"I think the sooner the better."

"And then what's going to happen?"

"He'll probably have her in his office and talk to her."

"What if she denies it?"

"At least it ought to put the fear of God in her. I mean, kids don't like being called into the principal's office. At least I never did."

"All right. First thing Monday. I feel like I'm snitching on her."

"You are snitching on her. But it's either that or risk landing in jail for contributing to the delinquency of a minor."

"Contributing *what*?"

"Whatever her fertile little mind thinks up."

"I wish this night was over with."

"Come on, drink up. We better get back in there."

"You go ahead, Woleski."

"I'm not leaving you here. Next thing you know Lolita will come waltzing into the bar and compromise you."

"How about if I hide out in the men's room?"

"Come on, I'll stay right by your side. If she asks you to dance again, I'll get rid of her."

"This is ridiculous, being terrorized by a teenager."

"You can handle it, Doug. You're tough."

"I used to think so."

"After the dance is over we'll go out and get something to eat, and tomorrow we'll laugh about this."

"And Monday morning I go to the principal."

"It's the only thing to do. It's not snitching, Doug— she's asking for it."

"I never told on anyone in my life."

"You've got to fight fire with fire."

"Where do you get these clichés?"

"I don't know. I just think of them."

"You'll stay by my side?"

"I'll stick to you like glue."

JILL GOT HOME feeling silly. Silly and young and something on the order of the belle of the ball. She was slightly intoxicated from the liquor and more than slightly intoxicated from the enjoyable encounter with Lacayo on the dance floor. The man had nearly died at her remark about sleeping in his underwear.

She took off her dress and hung it up. It was a great dress, the best she had ever owned. Too bad there was nowhere in Ethiopia to wear it. Hell, there were places in Ethiopia where she'd get arrested for wearing it.

She got out one of Lacayo's T-shirts and put it on to sleep in. Men's T-shirts were perfect to sleep in; she wondered why she had never thought of it before. She had purposely not said she was sleeping in his T-shirts, had purposely given him the impression it was probably his shorts she was sleeping in. Somehow shorts seemed a little sexier, a little more discomfiting for him to imagine. And she had a feeling he was imagining it, all right, maybe right at this moment.

She was in a good mood over Phaedra, too. The girl had danced all night, had managed to astound the popular girls with her success, and had conducted herself throughout as though it was second nature for her to be popular. Jill was proud of her.

She was still feeling high when she got into bed and reached over to turn off the lamp. Then she saw the diary and her mood instantly turned to remorse. She had no business having a good time at a high school dance. Susan should have been at that dance, enjoying her last days of high school. Susan should have had the new dress; Susan should have danced with the boys; Susan should be the one meeting the prince of her dreams. She even wondered if she'd still be playing the detective if she hadn't been attracted to Lacayo. If it had turned out boring, would she have given it up and flown back to Africa by now?

She tried to imagine what might have happened to Susan. She thought it was probably something like a beach party. She could picture a bunch of kids at the beach, Susan and the prince included. Maybe some horseplay in the water; maybe no one realizing what had happened at first, and then Susan not surfacing; maybe they all panicked and fled the beach. And, if so, they were probably greatly relieved when police had called it a suicide.

And they must be feeling terribly guilty about it. It's hard for kids to keep things to themselves. She knew that she would not be able to bear the knowledge.

She had to quit fooling around, quit flirting with the boys, quit the parties and dances, even quit hassling Lacayo. And if she didn't get anywhere soon, she should suggest her parents hire a private detective, someone who wouldn't be likely to fool around on the job, as she was doing.

Lacayo would still be there when it was all over.

Chapter Eight

The moon was full and cast its glow over the water. Out to sea the lights of a cruise ship could be seen, but none of the men huddled under the pier were looking at it. Most of them were asleep, whiskey breath mixing with salty air.

Jim Toland thought about going home. Sure, his dad had said not to show his face again until he had a steady job, but he knew his mom missed him. He was her baby, wasn't he? Didn't she always call him her baby? He had hated it when she called him that in front of his friends.

If he could get his clothes washed somewhere, get a pair of shoes, he ought to be able to hitch a ride north. He still had his Vermont driver's license. He could do all the driving to pay his way and maybe he'd get a few meals thrown in, too. With steady driving he could be back in Vermont in three days.

Florida wasn't for him. At first he thought it would be like Spring break all year round, but it hadn't worked out like that. The kids went home, and then it was all old people and no action. He tried to find work in Miami, but with all the illegal aliens flooding the area, willing to work for less than minimum wage, someone like him didn't have a chance. So he'd moved farther north to Lauderdale, but there was nothing for him there, either.

He figured Palm Cove would be good. Everyone here was rich, weren't they? He could do gardening, or at least wash cars. But by the time he got here, he was looking like a bum, just one pair of jeans and he didn't know where he'd left his basketball shoes.

He needed a shave, though. He was looking pretty scruffy, probably smelled, too. No chance of lifting a pack of razors from a convenience store, because the stores in Palm Cove, well, if you looked like he looked, they didn't even let you in the door.

Maybe if he called his mom she'd wire him some money. Just ten bucks would do it. Five. Just enough to get cleaned up and take the first ride out of town. He'd pay her back when he got a job.

The old guy next to him was snoring so damn loud Jim didn't even hear the kids at first. When he did, he looked up from underneath the brim of the squashed hat he'd found in someone's rubbish and that kept the sun off his head during the day.

He looked up and they were having so much fun that he thought maybe it was Spring break already and the kids were starting to come down again. He gave them a smile but they probably couldn't see it with him under the pier and it being dark and all.

He started to get up, ready to ask them where they were from, maybe see if they wanted to know where the action was, and then he saw that one of them was swinging something, and one of the others was yelling "Hit it out of the park" and it was coming at him fast and he thought maybe he ought to duck, but it was already too late.

Chapter Nine

He said something wonderful to me today. He said
I had potential! I don't know exactly what he
meant, but it's far and away the most unique thing
a boy has ever said to me. I just looked it up. It
means "existing in possibility." I hope that means
what I think it means. Well, I think he has possibilities, too. In fact I think there are great possibilities in our being together.

THE PHONE RANG and she grabbed it on the second
ring.

"You awake?"

She opened her eyes, felt a slight hangover and closed
them again. "No."

"It's a great day, I thought maybe you'd like to go to
the beach with us. You need to get your legs tanned, Jill.
You look like a Northerner."

"Go away," she mumbled.

"The water's eighty-two degrees."

"What are you doing up this early on a Sunday
morning, Alan?"

"It's almost noon."

"You didn't leave the dance any earlier than I did."

"You're wasting your weekend."

"I want to sleep."

"You've slept enough. Come on, bring your algebra book along if you want. We'll pick you up in fifteen minutes."

"I'll meet you there."

"You promise?"

She thought of her alternatives, and the beach sounded better. There was nothing to do on a Sunday except more laundry, and it wasn't likely Lacayo would show up at the same laundromat again. Anyway, hadn't she sworn off him last night? She'd give that some thought later.

"Yeah, I promise," she said.

"We'll be by the pier. The north side. Families hang out on the south side."

"I'll find you."

"Good. See you later."

SHE PICKED HER WAY between the bikini-clad girls on their color-coordinated beach towels. She was wearing the only bathing suit she owned, a one-piece tank suit in black that was more conducive to swimming than sunbathing. Sunbathing, however, wasn't a popular form of activity in third-world countries.

As she neared the pier, she could see some sort of activity going on beneath it. When she got closer she saw a group of men, some of them in uniforms. She wondered what so many police were doing on the beach on a Sunday morning.

She spotted Alan and David in the surf beside the pier, then saw Mark on the sand next to a cassette player. She dropped off her towel beside him, then headed for the water.

"Very nice," said Alan, eyeing her up and down.

"Quit acting like a child," said Jill, suddenly feeling exposed.

"A child?"

"Yes."

"If I were a child, I wouldn't even be looking."

"Try to achieve some subtlety, Singer."

He laughed and began splashing her with water.

She didn't protest as the water felt good. "What's going on over there?" she asked him.

"Didn't you hear?"

"Hear what?"

"I thought you were the one who read the newspapers."

"That's what I'd be doing right now if you hadn't dragged me down here."

"Nobody dragged you, Jill."

"So what happened?"

"There was another killing last night."

"One less homeless in the city of Palm Cove," said David.

"Right there?" asked Jill, suddenly feeling a chill although the water was warm.

"Right there," said Alan. "Want to go over and see?"

"Don't be ghoulish," she said.

"They chased us off, anyway," said David. "All we were trying to do was help."

"Have you ever seen a dead person?" Alan asked her.

"I've seen many," said Jill. "And many more starving to death."

"Oh, yeah—Africa—I forgot."

"You don't get used to it, though."

"Lot of kids, huh?" asked Alan, sounding more serious now.

She nodded. "I don't want to talk about it." It was too painful to talk about, and they were too young to hear it.

"Race you to the end of the pier," Alan challenged her, but instead of answering, she dove into the next wave and headed out.

He beat her by about ten lengths, which didn't surprise her. It had been a long time since she had been swimming, and though she was competent, she had never been proficient.

They were treading water when Mark showed up on the end of the pier and sat down, dangling his legs over the edge. David, who had gone further than them, circled around and swam back.

"You know that girl we were talking about in class last week?" Alan asked her.

"What girl?" she said, her stomach suddenly beginning to cramp.

"The one who committed suicide."

"Yeah, I remember," said Jill.

"This is where she did it," said Alan.

She felt herself shiver despite the warm water. "How could she drown here? It isn't even that far from shore."

"It is if you're not a good swimmer," said David.

Mark yelled down to them, "Her shoes were found right here, right next to where I'm sitting."

Without any warning, tears began to flood out of Jill's eyes. She had to get away from the spot, or she was going to go to pieces. She quickly took off for shore and could hear the boys behind her.

She tried to pull herself together before she reached the beach, but the thought of being in the very place where Susan had died was too much for her. When she got to the sand, she started running down the beach, away from the pier.

Alan caught up with her and pulled her to a stop, his hand on her wrist.

"Hey, what's the matter?"

"Nothing," she said, summoning all her control. "I just felt like some exercise."

"You're crying."

She smiled at him. "It's the salt water; it really stings."

"You're eyes are all red."

"I've never been in salt water before. I've never been in the ocean before."

Alan put his arm around her shoulder and steered her back in the direction of the pier. "You ought to get yourself some goggles," he said.

"Either that or stay out of the water."

"Never mind, it's time to work on your tan, anyway. Right now you look two-toned."

Jill looked through tears at where the police were still under the pier. Too many memories were surfacing—of starving people, of her younger sister, of the accounts in the newspaper of the men being beaten to death.

This was too difficult. It was really too difficult. Death had been all around her in Africa, and death was all around her here. She was beginning to understand why alcoholics needed a drink; it was to blot out the pain and be able to forget.

"Is this yours?" asked Trader, holding up a white sock with a red stripe around the top.

Doug looked up from the newspaper. "No. Mine are all white."

"I don't get it," said Trader. "How come everyone else loses socks at the laundry, and I always end up with extra ones."

"You're just lucky, Woleski."

"Why are you in such a bad mood?"

Doug shrugged.

"Come on, Lacayo, snap out of it."

"Why don't you put the ball game on?"

"Because I've decided to devote my day to putting you in a good mood."

"Don't do me any favors, Woleski."

"It's a beautiful day, eighty-seven degrees, manageable humidity, palm trees right outside our door, you've got clean laundry—what more could you ask for?"

"You're really Little Susie Sunshine today, aren't you?"

"Okay, so you were made a fool of at the dance last night. Does that mean you're going to sulk about it all day?"

Doug raised the paper to blot out his view of Trader.

"You really going to let a kid get to you?"

"Go sort your socks, Woleski."

"If you're wondering if I saw Lolita at the laundromat, the answer is no."

"Did you hear me ask?"

"You were wondering."

"Will you give me a break, Woleski?"

"I know what your problem is. You're jealous of Singer."

"She wasn't there with Singer."

"She was dancing with him most of the night."

"Woleski, the day I'm jealous of a high school boy—"

"Is Sunday. Today."

"You're a real comedian, you know it? How come Johnny Carson hasn't offered you his spot?"

"I'd just like to—"

"Buzz off!"

"You're starting to get on my nerves, Lacayo. What happened to you, anyway? You used to be fun."

"You're beginning to sound like a wife."

"I'm serious. You're beginning to sink into a depression."

Doug dropped the paper. "Someone's quiet for five minutes and you think it's a depression."

"Was it something in the paper?"

"Another homeless man was killed last night."

"People are dying all over the world; that's no reason for you personally to sink into despondency."

"Lay off, will you?"

"Are you telling me that that's what's depressing you?"

"I'm not depressed."

"Right."

Doug shook his head. "I don't understand it, though. A pretty, quiet little town like this, you wouldn't think something like that would happen."

"It's always the pretty, quiet little towns where mass murderers go to work."

"You know what really gets to me, Trader? We talk about the killings in class, and the kids really don't care."

"It's not real to them. They see it on TV all the time. They see worse in the movies."

"I get the feeling they think homeless people don't count. I've never seen a more spoiled bunch of kids."

"It's not just the kids, Doug. If everyone really cared, something would be done about them."

"I don't like it."

"Come on, Doug, there were a hell of a lot more homeless in Chicago."

"Yeah, but there you saw the progression. You saw poor people and then you saw destitute people and then you saw the homeless. Here you just see the rich and the homeless and nothing in between."

"We're in between."

"Yeah, but we don't count. We're just teachers. We're like the people who do their gardening and clean their houses. And we either live out of town, or in their guest houses."

"What do I detect here, a social conscience?"

"You used to have one."

"Never! You're mistaking me for someone else."

Doug started to smile. "Yeah, you're right. I don't know why it's getting to me, Trader. Just ignore it and get me a beer."

"Now you're sounding like your old self."

JILL WAS DEPRESSED. She couldn't concentrate on her homework and she couldn't concentrate on TV. Alan called her around five and tried to cheer her up. She appreciated the effort, but it didn't work. She tried to read some more of Susan's diary, but that sunk her into a deeper depression and she finally gave it up.

She felt like giving it all up. She was tired of masquerading as a student, tired of spending futile time getting nowhere when she could be back in Africa doing some good, tired of falling for a man who thought she was a child and panicked whenever she came near him. She couldn't do this alone. She ought to go to the police, tell them her suspicions, and...right, and what? Tell them her sister wasn't suicidal? They'd laugh her out of the station. They had murders to investigate; they wouldn't be interested in an alleged suicide where they'd already closed the case.

She needed a friend. An ally. She needed Mr. Lacayo on her side. If she had any guts at all, she'd go over to his house again and this time not leave until she told him the truth. The worst that could happen would be that he'd still reject her. In which case she'd drop out of school, talk her parents into hiring a detective and go back to where she belonged.

And the best? Well, if the best happened, she wouldn't feel so alone anymore. It was hard pretending to be someone else all the time. If he knew, she'd have someone to talk to, to be herself with. And anyway, not being able to see him was driving her up the wall!

SHE MARCHED UP the driveway and banged on the door with her fist, feeling determined. If they didn't let her in, she was prepared to break down the door or throw a rock through the window. She had backed down twice, and that's more than she usually backed down from anything. Game time was over and she wanted to get down to serious business.

The roommate opened the door. Cool gray eyes scrutinized her for a moment and then a devilish grin raised his mustache a notch.

She made a calculated move to go around him and into the house, but a muscular arm shot out and blocked her way.

"Not wearing any of my clothes today?" he asked her, the look in his eyes wicked.

"I might be," she said, just as coolly.

She tried to duck under his arm, but he seemed to expand to fill the doorway.

"You're driving my buddy nuts, you know," he said, and she thought she detected a look of admiration in his eyes. She was quite capable of imagining that, though.

"I'm not going away," she said, in the same conversational tone of voice he had used.

He turned his head and yelled out, "It's Lolita, Dougie," and then he moved aside so that she could enter.

As soon as she was in the entryway she saw Mr. Lacayo in the living room to her left. He was sitting on the couch in the midst of newspapers and giving a pretty good imitation of a person frozen in place.

She walked into the room as far as the coffee table, reached into her pocket, took out her passport, and threw it on Lacayo's lap. He transferred his dazed look to his roommate.

"Open it," she said to Lacayo, not sounding anything like a teenager, or an innocent or the daughter of missionaries. She spoke in the tone she used to give orders, and they were usually obeyed.

"Wake up, Lacayo, it's the children's hour," said the roommate, who had circled around and was now leaning against the wall. "Anyway, you got to admire her guts."

Lacayo almost smiled. "So you have a passport, so what? It figures since you've been living out of the country."

"You want me to throw her out of here?" asked the roommate, but he didn't sound serious.

Jill crossed her arms and glared at Lacayo. "Will you just look at it, please?"

Lacayo slowly opened the passport and stared down at it for a moment. "Lousy picture," he observed.

"Maybe we should call the cops," said the roommate.

Jill turned around and said, "Shut up!"

"Sorry, nothing personal," said the roommate.

Jill turned back to Lacayo. "Never mind the picture, look at the date of birth."

Lacayo held up the passport. "It says Jill Peters. They got you down at school as Wyckoff."

The roommate snorted. "A phony name? This is getting more bizarre by the moment."

"Will you please read my date of birth, or do I have to read it for you?"

He looked at the passport again and then looked back up. "Not bad. Better than the phony ID I had when I was a kid. Do you get served with this?"

The roommate moved in for a look. "Very nice, it looks like a professional job."

"It's not phony. I happen to be twenty-seven."

"And you're still in high school?" asked the roommate. "Hey, Doug, I thought you said she was intelligent."

Jill began to smile. "You think I'm intelligent?"

Lacayo grinned. "For a high school kid."

"Could someone please explain what's happening?" asked the roommate.

"I happen to have a master's degree," said Jill, still smiling at her teacher.

"Just ignore me; I'm not even here," said the roommate.

"Can I trust him?" Jill asked Lacayo, nodding her head in the direction of his roommate.

"Yeah, you can trust Trader. Trader, meet Jill. She's twenty-seven, not seventeen."

"Almost twenty-eight," said Jill.

Lacayo's grin was almost splitting his face. "What a relief. I was beginning to think I was going through a mid-life crisis, and I'm only twenty-nine. Almost thirty."

Trader said, "If she's not jailbait, I guess I can close the door."

They were still smiling at each other when Trader came back and took a seat on the couch. "Since we're all speaking, might I inquire about my laundry?"

"Shut up, Trader," said Lacayo. His grin faded a little. "I don't get it," he said. "You came all the way from Ethiopia just to go to high school? Or was that a lie, too?" He opened up the passport and took another look. "No, I see it's stamped from Ethiopia."

"Maybe she's some Board of Education spy," said Trader.

"They don't have a branch in Ethiopia," said Lacayo.

"Could be Drug Enforcement."

Jill forced her eyes away from Lacayo and looked at Trader. "I happen to work for the World Health Organization."

Lacayo chuckled. "What've we got, an outbreak of the plague in Palm Cove?"

"I need your help," said Jill.

"You got it," said Trader. "I don't want to catch whatever it is."

Jill sighed and became serious. "If you two could knock off your Laurel and Hardy act for a moment..."

"Not yet," said Lacayo. "If this is going to turn serious, I think I need a drink."

"Hell, I *know* I need a drink," said Trader.

"I wouldn't mind a beer if you have one," said Jill, thinking it might do something for her headache.

"*If* we have one?" said Trader. "Just name your brand. If you're really legal, that is."

"I'm legal."

"Okay, okay," said Trader, going into the kitchen. Jill could hear the refrigerator door opening.

"Have a seat," said Lacayo.

"Thanks, Mr. Lacayo," she said, pulling a chair up to the coffee table.

"Oh, no," he said, shaking his head. "After all you've put me through, for God's sake call me Doug."

"I think of you as Mr. Lacayo."

"Then start doing some rethinking. I knew there was something about you. I just knew it."

"You did not," said Jill. "I had you completely fooled."

"Not completely."

"Then why did you bolt from the laundromat? And almost have a heart attack when I showed up here? To say nothing of the expression on your face when we were dancing."

"'Cause my mind wasn't believing what my body was telling me."

"What was your body telling you?"

"I can't wait to hear this," said Trader, coming back into the room and handing them each a can of beer.

"What I can't believe," said Doug, "is you're twenty-seven, *almost* twenty-eight, and you're coming on to Alan Singer. I think that's illegal."

"Like you have a right to talk," said Trader, enjoying it all hugely.

"I like Alan," said Jill.

"Obviously," said Doug, sounding somewhat miffed.

"And I thought he could help me."

"Oh, I noticed him helping you all right, particularly in study hall."

Jill almost smiled at the thought that he was sounding jealous of Alan. She decided not to mention the fact that she and Alan had gotten to be friends.

"I don't get it," said Trader. "Why would anyone want to go to high school twice? It's like my worst nightmare."

"That's how I felt in algebra the first day," admitted Jill. "I couldn't remember the simplest things."

"Until Singer started helping you out," said Doug.

"He's very good at math," said Jill.

"He's some kind of mathematical genius," said Trader.

"And here I finally thought I had a student who read the newspapers," said Doug, in an obvious attempt to get the subject off Alan.

"I read the newspapers," said Jill.

"Yeah, but you're a fake student."

"And lucky for you, I'd say," said Trader.

She hated to bring the good feeling to an end. "My sister was Susan Peters," she said.

Trader said, "Wasn't she the one who—"

"Yeah," said Doug.

"Oh, hell, I'm sorry," said Trader. "So what're you doing, taking her place?"

"If she were taking her place, Woleski, she wouldn't be using an assumed name."

"Maybe Wyckoff's her married name," countered Trader.

Doug looked disturbed at that suggestion. "Are you married?" he asked her.

"No, I'm not, but that has nothing to do with anything. I'm trying to find out what happened to Susan."

"The police said it was suicide," said Doug.

"I don't believe it."

"I don't remember seeing you at the funeral," said Doug.

"I didn't even find out about it until after she was buried. There was no way to get hold of me."

"That's rough," he said, his eyes sympathetic.

"I understand what you're feeling," said Trader. "It's hard to believe when someone you love commits suicide."

"Look, are you guys going to turn me in?"

"To whom?" asked Doug.

"The principal. The school authorities."

"Far be it from me to get anyone kicked out of high school who's as bright a student as you are."

"Hey, I'm not a snitch," said Trader.

"Look," said Jill. "Number one, my sister was a good swimmer. She was on the high school swimming team in Michigan."

"You're talking lakes," said Trader. "The ocean can get tricky."

"I just don't think that swimmers jump off piers to commit suicide," said Jill. "The natural inclination would be to swim."

Doug was nodding his head.

"Number two, she wrote me letters all the time and she sounded happy. And believe me, when Susan wasn't happy about something, it was me she complained to."

"She didn't leave a note or anything, did she?" asked Doug.

Jill shook her head. "And she was the kind who would. She was always writing. Which brings me to number three—she left a diary that my mom found in Susan's drawer. Mom was afraid to read it, but I went through it for any suicidal thoughts, and there just weren't any."

"This happens in teenage suicide," said Doug. "Parents saying they can't understand it, friends saying the kid had no problems—"

"She was in love," said Jill.

"And a lot of people kill themselves over love."

"I didn't come here for an argument," said Jill. "You're not telling me anything I don't already know."

"Sorry," said Doug, "I'm just playing devil's advocate. And I'm so damn used to arguing with you."

"She was in love with some guy in her civics class."

"I see," said Doug.

"No name—she just refers to him as the prince."

"You think this guy had something to do with it?" asked Trader.

"No, not really, but I think he might know something. I just think that if there was some freak accident, or any kind of accident, the boy—or maybe a group of kids—would be afraid to come forward. And the police calling it a suicide would let them off the hook."

"I don't know," said Trader. "If you thought it was foul play, that would be a different matter."

"I don't want anyone punished," said Jill. "It's just that my parents are going to blame themselves for the rest of their lives if they think Susan killed herself. I just want to find out who the prince is, see if he knows anything, and then get back to my job."

Doug looked at Trader. "Alan Singer."

"He's a prince all right," said Trader.

"You saw them together?" asked Jill.

Doug shook his head.

"I don't see Alan as the prince," said Jill. "Susan was shy, kind of quiet—I don't think she was his type."

"Unlike yourself," said Doug.

"I'm just a challenge to him," said Jill. "And that's only because I don't give a damn what the kids think of me."

"Or the teachers," said Trader.

"If you're so worried about your laundry," Jill told him, "it's in the trunk of my car. Dirty."

"So this is why you brought up the subject of teen-age suicide in class," said Doug. "It seemed a little heavy at the time."

"Did you notice the reaction it got?" Jill asked him.

"I suppose you think it was out of guilt."

"It looked that way."

He shook his head. "It was a natural reaction. Pick any class in the school and they would have reacted the same way."

"So what are you doing by way of investigation besides wearing Doug's undies?" asked Trader.

"I was planning on dating all the boys in the class who could conceivably be the prince," said Jill.

"You've been dating high school boys?" asked Doug, sounding incredulous.

"I know, it's probably against the law," said Jill, "but I didn't try to seduce them. And there was really only one so far. Some of them already have girlfriends, and one refused to go out with a girl who called him for a date."

"Who was the one, Singer?" asked Trader.

"No. Peter."

"That guy's got a bad reputation," said Doug.

"Come on, Lacayo," said Jill, "you really think I can't handle a teenager?"

"She probably scared the hell out of him, just like she did you," said Trader.

"So how can we help?" asked Doug.

"It helps just to have someone to talk to," said Jill. "And I thought maybe you knew something I didn't know. There must have been talk after her death."

Doug shook his head. "You hear anything, Woleski?"

"Sure, but nothing out of the ordinary."

"If I could just find out who the prince was," said Jill.

"Dating habits of teenagers," said Doug.

"What?"

"I could do a study. I could tell the class I'm doing a sociological study on dating habits of teenagers. Strictly confidential, of course."

"I don't get it," said Trader.

Doug was nodding his head. "I could make out these forms—who they've dated in the past year, who the boys have asked out and been turned down by, who they've been interested in and why, et cetera, et cetera."

"Some of those guys aren't going to remember who they asked out last week," said Trader.

"And the prince is not likely to write down Susan's name," said Jill.

"They're not as smart as they think they are," said Doug. "This diary, does it give any dates?"

Jill nodded.

"So look, the least it will do is eliminate most of the boys. And something might turn up."

"I suppose," said Jill.

"Do you have any better ideas besides dating the entire senior class?"

"I don't know how you're going to square this with current events," said Trader.

"Oh, hell, they're not interested in current events anyway. Jill's the only one interested in that."

"And I'm a fake," said Jill.

"Exactly."

"If he's one of the jocks, maybe I could do something," said Trader.

"I don't know. Ask around, I guess."

"Maybe you could take one of the boys into your confidence," said Jill. "One you trust who's been going steady for the past year."

"Get myself an informant?" Trader asked her.

"I guess you wouldn't want to do that."

"I don't like informants myself," said Trader, "but there's one little sneak who does the broad jump whom I wouldn't mind turning."

"Give it a try," said Doug.

"Yeah, I will."

Jill sat back in the chair and smiled with relief. "You don't know how good it is to have someone to talk to."

"You could've told us sooner," said Doug.

She gave him a look of disbelief. "What do you think I was trying to do when I came over here the first time? You were so scared, you wouldn't have listened."

"He's been freaking out," said Trader.

Jill grinned. "Oh, really?"

"I thought you were going to get me fired, that's all," said Doug.

"And if you swallow that, he'll tell you another one," said Trader.

Jill said, "Listen, I don't think I should hang around here any longer. My car's parked right out front, and if someone sees it—"

Trader slapped his forehead. "Three of my students live on this block."

"And two of mine," said Doug.

"I'd better get out of here."

"Let's all get out of here," said Trader. "You want to meet somewhere out of town where we won't be seen? Have a little adult company?"

Jill looked at Doug who appeared to be about to strangle Trader. "Sure, I'd love to," she said.

Trader finally seemed to catch Doug's mood. "I'll have to cut out early, though."

Jill could see that Doug was relieved by that, but she wasn't. Now that he knew the truth, she was a little scared of being alone with him. Coming on to him from the safety of being underage no longer applied.

"Don't worry," said Doug, "I'm not out for revenge."

"Revenge?"

"Yeah, revenge. For *Lolita*, for that crack about sleeping in my underwear—"

Jill eyed him with enjoyment. "The book was purely accidental."

"And the underwear remark?"

"Definitely calculated."

Chapter Ten

We're going to date, but in secret. I LOVE the idea!! I always wanted a wonderful, romantic secret. I thought he'd try to kiss me but he didn't. I wasn't going to let him, anyway, but I wish he'd tried. He has wonderful self-control!!

DOUG TURNED DOWN the volume on the car radio. "What do you think of her?"

There was silence for a moment, and then Trader said, "Interesting."

"What does that mean?"

"Interesting? It means of interest."

Doug turned around to look out the back window. "Slow down, you're going to lose her."

"She's right on my tail. In fact she's going to be climbing my bumper any second if she doesn't slow down."

"Interesting? What do you mean by that?"

"Will you relax, Lacayo? You should be relieved she's not seventeen. Anything else is unimportant."

"What else?"

"Anything."

"You didn't like something about her?"

"I barely know her, Lacayo. I mean, she went from being Lolita to the Avenger out of Africa in just a few seconds. It takes some getting used to."

"Yeah." He turned around to look again. "Slow down a little, huh?"

"I'm going the exact speed limit, what do you want?"

"You know, Woleski, you could've stayed home."

"You don't want me around?"

"I'd kind of like to be alone with her."

"I figured you needed a chaperone."

"Yeah, right."

"We'll have a few drinks, relax a little, and then I'll cut out. She can drive you home."

Doug tried to resist the temptation to turn around again and lost. "I think you're losing her."

"I don't think you could lose her if you tried, Lacayo."

"What do you mean by that?"

"I mean, she's always turning up, isn't she? If she could follow you home without you seeing her, she can certainly follow us to Lauderdale."

"Do you like her?"

"Sure. What's not to like? It takes guts posing as a high school student."

"What if she thinks of me as her teacher?"

"I doubt whether she ever thought of you as a teacher."

"She called me Mr. Lacayo."

"She's used to thinking of you that way."

"You know, Woleski, this is going to sound stupid, but I have a feeling we'd be perfect together."

"Why, because she argues with you in class?"

"Because we're both interested in the same things."

"I didn't know you were interested in world health."

"Of course I'm interested. Who's not?"

Trader gave him a droll look.

"She cares about people. She's trying to make a difference."

"Don't get on a crusade here, Lacayo. We're going to have a few drinks, have some fun—"

"She's not behind you anymore."

"She's one car back; everything's under control."

IT WAS WALL-TO-WALL CARS and they had to park a few blocks from the ocean. Jill pulled in right behind them and Doug started to relax. Twenty-four hours ago he never would've dreamed this could happen. "Where'd all the kids come from?" he asked Trader.

"Spring break."

"Already?"

"They stagger it now. Some of the schools must already be off."

"Are you sure you're not going to see anyone you know here?" Jill asked them. "I don't want to get you guys in trouble."

"I doubt it," said Trader. "No one I know has any business out partying on a Sunday night. Anyway, this place gets strictly a college crowd."

"If you do see anyone you know," she said, "I'll act like I'm not with you."

When they got to the bar Trader favored, kids were out the door and all over the sidewalk. They started to push their way in, but a big guy with a ponytail asked to see Jill's ID.

She took out her passport and handed it to him, but he wasn't impressed. "Got any other ID?" he asked her.

"That's perfectly valid identification," Jill told him.

"Got a driver's license?"

She took out her wallet and pulled out a driver's license.

"What kind of driver's license is this?"

"International."

He still wasn't impressed.

"What is this nonsense?" asked Trader. "She's an exchange teacher from Africa and you're giving her a hard time? I'd like to speak to the manager."

"She doesn't look twenty-one," said the bouncer.

"Neither do you," said Trader.

"Maybe we should just go," suggested Doug, not thinking it worth the effort when there were a dozen more bars just like it in the area.

"No, I want to see the manager," said Trader.

"Maybe you'd like to see my American Express," said Jill.

"Yeah, I'd like to see that," said the bouncer.

Jill handed her entire wallet to the guy and he flipped through it. "Okay," he said at last, "go on in."

Once in the bar, Jill looked around and said, "This is ridiculous. We're the oldest ones here and he's giving *me* a hard time?"

"He thought you were being a smartass with the passport," said Trader.

"Then he's ignorant," said Jill.

"He's probably never seen a passport," said Trader.

Doug was already feeling a little uncomfortable. The bar was eighty percent guys and they were all looking Jill over. A couple of them were already hitting on her. And she was joking around with them as though it was okay. She was a little friendlier than he thought she ought to be, but maybe that came from living out of the country.

Most of the kids were congregating around the bar or else were on the dance floor, and Trader managed to find them a table at the back. It was still crowded and noisy, but if they shouted they could be heard.

Trader left for the bar to get them each a beer, and Jill said, "You want to dance, Mr. Lacayo?"

"Cut out the *Mr.*, will ya?"

"Doug doesn't seem right."

"Doug is absolutely right."

She gave him a smile, a personal kind of smile, the kind that used to drive him nuts in class when he thought she was seventeen, but now seemed just right. "Let's dance, Doug," she said.

He listened for a moment to the music. It was too fast, not the kind of music he could dance to. "Not to this," he said.

"This is one of my favorite songs."

He listened a little more. It was the kind of music he really hated. Trader appeared right then with the beer and it let him off the hook as far as dancing went because they were all lifting their glasses to Trader's toast—"Here's to Lolita."

A couple of college boys stopped by the table and seemed to know Trader.

"Hey," said Trader, "these guys were on my team last year," then introduced Jim and Craig to Doug, and introducing Jill as his visiting sister.

Craig made some joke about the lack of family resemblance, then asked Jill to dance. Doug was sure she'd refuse, but she got up and the next thing he knew they were dancing.

He kept stealing glances at them on the dance floor and they looked good together. Okay, the guy was a few years younger than she was, but they were both terrific dancers and she seemed to be enjoying herself. He thought the whole purpose of her coming to his house had been to get to know him; he didn't see why she had to go dance with someone else.

Jim was sitting at their table now and was discussing football with Trader. Doug tuned out the football talk, glad that soon Trader would be leaving and he and Jill could get to know each other. At least with her it wouldn't be football talk.

He kept waiting for the music to end so that Jill would come back to the table. The song seemed to go on and on and he couldn't make out the lyrics, but the melody was sure monotonous. When the song finally ended and a slow tune began, Doug looked around and saw Jill and Craig heading back for the table.

He got up and met them halfway, saying to Jill, "Want to dance to this one?"

"Just let me drink a little of that beer," she said. "You really build up a thirst dancing."

He stood by the table as she downed the beer, Jim and Craig and Trader now all discussing football, then she took his hand and they headed onto the floor. They practically had the space to themselves as the kids didn't seem to care for the slow tune.

He held her loosely, one hand on her back and the other holding her hand. She smiled at him. "This isn't as much fun as the school dance," she said, her eyes laughing at him.

"I guess you know how uncomfortable you made me."

"Oh, yes—I was well aware of that," she said.

"I thought you were trying to get me fired."

"Not fired, just fired up."

"Well, you succeeded."

"And then you disappeared somewhere."

"In the bar with Trader. He talked me into reporting you to the principal on Monday."

She grinned. "You still going to do it?"

"Hell no!"

"You really would've reported me?"

"I tell you, you had me running scared."

Jill laughed. "If kids only knew what power they have. I wouldn't have dared do something like that in high school."

"Oh, once in a while you get a wild girl—"

"You thought I was wild?"

"I couldn't figure you out. You were so bright in class, but then you showed up at my house."

"You didn't give me a chance to explain."

"How was I to know you had something to explain?"

"Trying to talk to you alone was really frustrating."

"You think *you* were frustrated? I felt like I was being attacked from all sides. Seeing you in my laundromat? Carrying *Lolita*? I almost had a heart attack."

"The book wasn't intentional. I had no idea you'd be there, anyway."

"Look at it from my point of view."

"I am, and it's funny."

He couldn't help grinning. "Yeah, I guess it is. In retrospect."

She moved in a little closer to him and this time he didn't push her away. In fact he put both arms around her, but left enough distance so that they could still talk.

"Can I tell you a secret?" he asked her.

"Sure. I've told you mine."

"This is something I've never told anybody."

"Good, let's hear it."

"You gotta promise not to tell Woleski."

"Why would I tell him?"

"Just promise."

"Word of honor."

He leaned into her ear and whispered, "I hate sports."

She gave him a quizzical look. "How can you coach baseball and hate sports?"

"It's not easy."

"But why do it?"

He shrugged. "It's no worse than teaching."

"You don't like teaching?"

"Not that bunch of spoiled brats."

"Then why don't you get out of it?"

"I'm going to."

"I don't like baseball much anymore," she said, "but I used to love it when I was a kid."

"Me too," said Doug, "but now it seems rather childish."

"And slow," she said, "and boring."

He gave her a pleased look. "Exactly."

"Football's different, though," she said.

"Football?"

"It doesn't seem childish like baseball. It seems more of an adult game."

"Maybe on the surface," he conceded.

"You don't like football?"

"I told you; I don't like sports. None of them."

"You really don't like football?"

He grinned at her. "What's to like? It bores me to death."

She looked doubtful. "I love football."

"You're putting me on."

"I aspired to being the first female Big Ten quarterback."

"You?"

"You don't have to sound so condescending. I was a damn good football player."

"Okay, *playing* it was fun," Doug admitted. "But watching it is boring as hell."

"The one thing I really miss in Africa is not being able to watch the NFL games," she said.

"No football over there?"

She shook her head.

"Sounds like my kind of place."

"I don't believe you, you know."

"What?"

"I don't believe you really don't like sports. You're just saying that because you think women don't know anything about sports. I bet I know as much as you do."

"Great." And just when he'd been thinking they'd be so compatible.

The music turned fast again and Doug led her back to the table. The boys were still there, and Doug drew up another chair. Within seconds Jill was joining in with their football talk and any hope that she had been kidding about how much she knew about sports was instantly dashed. She was a little out of date, but she knew her stuff.

Doug looked at his watch and wondered when Woleski was going to cut out and leave them alone. It didn't appear to be anytime soon. Every time he caught Woleski's eye, he tried to give him a meaningful look, but meaningful looks went right over Woleski's head. Doug finally got up and got them all another beer.

After about another twenty minutes the boys finally left to join their friends, and Doug figured that Woleski would finally take the hint and leave. Instead he continued the football talk with Jill, who didn't seem bothered by the fact that she and Doug weren't talking anymore.

It was finally Jill who said, "Listen, I'm going to have to cut out. I've got a test in English tomorrow and I have to study for it."

"What for?" Trader asked her.

"I'm not prepared."

"So what?" asked Trader. "You're not a real student, either. Does it really matter if you flunk it?"

"It matters to me," said Jill.

"If I were in your shoes, I sure as hell wouldn't study," said Trader.

Doug said, "Would you mind dropping me off? I'd like to get started on that sociological survey we were talking about."

"We can leave in a little while," said Trader.

"I want to leave now," said Doug.

Trader finally got the message and winked at him. But then Trader often was dense.

THEY HELD HANDS on the way to Jill's car and she was feeling good. Just being out having a good time with a couple of adults had made all the difference. She no longer felt isolated, now that she had a couple of friends. And maybe one was going to be more than a friend. She'd also enjoyed the football talk, although, judging by how much Doug had added to the conversation, she guessed he hadn't been kidding about not liking sports. She'd reserve judgment on that, though, until she got to know him better. In her experience all normal men liked sports.

As soon as she started up the car, the station with the rock music she kept tuned to came on loud, and she saw Doug wince. She turned it down low enough so that they could talk.

"I like your roommate," she said.

"He's been my best friend since we were kids."

"Where'd you grow up?"

"Chicago."

"Yeah? I grew up in Michigan."

"We were practically neighbors."

"You don't know what a treat tonight was for me. It's very wearing spending all your time with teenagers."

"Tell me about it."

"But you don't have to pretend to be their age. And you've got Trader to talk to."

"All he talks about are sports and women."

"That beats talking about high school boys."

"The boys seem to like you."

"Sure, I'm a challenge. I don't care if they like me, so naturally they do. How about you? You date a lot?"

"Not really."

"Why not?"

"You don't meet many women when you're a teacher."

She doubted that. She doubted that any guy who looked as good as Doug had trouble meeting women. It sounded as though he wasn't dating anyone, though, and that was fine with her. "What do you think of the latest killing?" she asked him.

He grinned at her. "We don't have to discuss current events out of school."

"I'm interested in current events."

"Good. So am I. I'm outraged by the killings, but it's the homeless problem that's the real disgrace."

"It seems strange a place like Palm Cove would have homeless."

"They come up from Miami. Or maybe down from the North, who knows?"

"At least they're not starving to death," said Jill.

"They're not eating regularly, I can tell you that."

"Can't they get unemployment? Or welfare?"

"I thought you'd care about them," said Doug, sounding disappointed in her.

"At least you don't see starving children," said Jill. "And I do care about them, but somehow the homeless I've seen here don't look anywhere near as bad off as the starving people in Ethiopia. These people at least have opportunities. There is work. There is food. There is certainly an abundance of water."

"Sorry," he said. "I know it's nothing like Ethiopia. It's just that in this country, you don't expect to see any of that. There's so much money, so many resources, there shouldn't be homeless. Unless from choice."

She turned off in Palm Cove and Doug immediately ducked down in the seat.

"Getting a little paranoid?" she asked him.

"I just don't want to be seen."

She reached over and tickled his ribs.

"Don't do that!"

"No one's going to see you in the dark."

"Look, I'm not worried about being fired. No one's going to fire me when they find out you're an imposter. But if we're seen together, you're not going to find out what happened to your sister.''

"It's my welfare you're worried about?"

"Yes."

"Okay. You're forgiven. But if you sat up and turned your head away from the window, no one's going to recognize you."

"Your car's too recognizable."

"This?"

"For this town."

"Well, you can relax, because we're on your street. Should I pull into the driveway?"

"Out in front's fine."

She pulled to a stop and turned off the lights. Doug sat up and reached for the door handle.

"Aren't you going to kiss me good-night?" she asked, keeping the tone light.

"Here?"

Such paranoia was too much for her. "Good night, Mr. Lacayo," she said, switching the tone to cool.

All he said was a hurried "Good night" and then he was out of the car and running up the driveway. And was she angry he hadn't said anything about seeing her again? Damn right she was. What did he think, a group of interested school board members were hiding in his bushes and monitoring his moves?

She burned rubber escaping from his house.

GOD, THAT WAS chicken behavior on his part. He'd been dying to kiss her, and instead he had acted like the worst kind of paranoic. Okay, so he hadn't been as happy with her at the end of the evening as he had been at the first. So she had flirted with the college students, so what? And was he supposed to punish her because she liked football? Millions of people liked football. It wasn't even football season, so what difference did it make? And okay, so she liked to argue with him, he had already known that. He liked arguing with her, too, only he thought she was wrong about the homeless people. But to be perfectly fair, he knew conditions were far worse in Ethiopia than he could even imagine.

He hadn't even said "I'll see you tomorrow" or "What are you doing Saturday night?" or anything else. He was taking her for granted, and they hadn't even dated yet. What he ought to do was call her, only he didn't have her number and she wouldn't be home yet.

He looked up the only Wyckoff in the phone book, gave them a call, explained that he was Jill's civics teacher, and they gave him her number. He'd take a shower while he gave her time to get home, and then he'd call up and apologize.

When he got out of the shower, Trader was already home and watching the news.

"I figured you were alone when I didn't see her car," said Trader. "How'd you make out?"

"I didn't 'make out,' Woleski."

"And here I figured—"

"I *know* what you figured."

"You were hot for her, you find out she's legal, and you don't do anything about it?"

"We haven't even dated yet."

"This ain't high school, Lacayo. Anyway, how the hell do you plan on dating her without being caught?"

"Out of town."

"It better be *far* out of town, buddy, because everyone in this town who fools around goes out of town."

"So what's the worst that can happen? We get caught, that's all. It's not like she's really seventeen."

"Yeah, but she's not going to appreciate it if you mess up her chances of finding out what really happened to her sister."

"I got to work on that questionnaire to give the kids tomorrow."

"I'll help you."

"You know, I really like her."

"I could tell. Listen, even I liked her. She knows more about football than any woman I ever met."

"Aside from that, I think we're perfect together."

"What do you mean, aside from that? That's what makes it perfect."

"I think we have the same sensibilities."

"Just don't get carried away, Lacayo. Remember, she is a woman."

"Meaning what?"

"Meaning that when you try to see similarities between the two of you, you're way off base. It's like finding similarities with Martians. We like to believe we have something in common with them, but we're two different species."

"Men and women happen to be the same species, Woleski."

"You got your head buried in the sand, Lacayo? They're aliens, and until you understand that you'll never understand women."

"And you understand them, I suppose."

"Listen, I've had more experience than you."

"You've had more sex, that's all."

"I'm just saying you're expecting too much. You're setting yourself up for a fall."

"I'd like to get serious about someone, do you mind?"

"Next thing I'll be hearing you want to get married."

"So what's so bad about that?"

"Nothing, if you like being a second-class citizen."

"I don't get you, Woleski. You think the ideal situation is still having a roommate at thirty?"

"We can always hire a cleaning lady."

"I can clean, myself. I'd like companionship."

"Don't give me that. You get companionship from men—what you want is steady sex."

"I consider that to be part of companionship with the right woman."

"Where'd you get these ideas? I don't remember your parents' marriage being made in heaven."

"They get along."

"It's the monotony. It's the same woman every morning and every night and all weekend. It's the lack of variety."

"I'm more monogamous than you are."

"No one's monogamous. That's just something women made up and it's never worked."

"Wait'll you're sixty and still trying to get women."

"Paul Newman's older than that. You think he'd have trouble picking up women?"

"Paul Newman has hair."

"You really know how to hurt a guy," said Woleski, turning up the sound on the TV.

Doug grabbed the phone and carried it into the kitchen and closed the door.

IT WAS ALMOST MIDNIGHT when the phone rang and she still hadn't finished reading.

"What're you doing?" Doug asked her.

"Reading *Macbeth*."

"Sounds like fun."

"Oh, absolutely—just what I feel like reading after a few beers. It keeps putting me to sleep."

"You ought to be able to fake the test."

"I haven't read it since high school."

"Listen, I'm sorry I was so paranoid in the car."

"You should be."

"It's not that I didn't want to kiss you."

"Ummm."

"I mean it."

"That's okay. I'm not one of those girls who kiss on a first date."

"No?"

"Actually I'm lying. But that wasn't even a date."

"You kiss on first dates?"

"It's hard to remember, it's been so long since I've dated."

"For me it depends on how much I like the person."

"Do I take that to mean you don't like me, Mr. Lacayo?"

"Was that your Lolita voice?"

"You recognized it."

"I like you. It's just a relief to know I like you and you're not seventeen."

"What you're saying is, you liked a high school kid."

"I liked a *fake* high school kid."

"What if I weren't a fake?"

"You are, though, so the question's moot."

"You might've liked me at seventeen."

"I doubt it."

"You've never had a student who appealed to you?"

"No."

"I don't believe you."

"I don't think of them that way. I think of them as kids and that way I don't get interested."

"You were thinking of me as a kid and you got interested."

"That's 'cause you were different."

"I wasn't that different. All it seems to take to interest you is someone who reads the paper."

"That's not all."

"Oh? What else interested you?"

"The way you argued with me. Which you can stop now, you know."

"I like arguing with you."

"I meant you can stop it in class."

"No way. That class would be totally boring if we didn't argue."

"Thanks a lot."

"Okay. I'll stop arguing in class if we can argue some other time."

"That's what I was getting to."

"It was taking you too long," said Jill.

"I want to see you again."

"I'm glad to hear it."

"I'd like to date you."

"You sound like a high school boy."

"It's still called dating, isn't it?"

"Maybe there's another school dance you can take me to."

"The thing is, Jill, we're going to have to date secretly."

Something flashed in her mind. "That sounds like my sister and the prince."

"I beg your pardon?"

"They were dating secretly."

"In our case, it's a necessity."

"Put that on the test."

"What?"

"About dating secretly. Ask the students if any of them have dated secretly and why."

"Yeah, I'm going to do that as soon as I hang up."

"Okay."

"Okay, what?"

"Okay, when are we going to start dating secretly?"

"I was wondering," said Doug.

"Yes?"

"I didn't have your phone number so I called the Wyckoffs. Why is your number different from theirs?"

"Because I'm staying in their garage apartment."

"Alone?"

"All alone. Their gardener used to live here."

"So I could come over there?"

"That's not a very good idea."

"I think it's a great idea. I can bring some food; we can get to know each other."

"Alan comes by a lot."

"Alan Singer?"

"He and his friends stop by."

"They come over to your apartment and you live alone?"

"It's all right, Doug, they think I'm seventeen."

"I don't think it's all right. I know what boys are like at seventeen."

"What are they like?"

"Horny."

"It's not like that. Alan and I are friends. He likes to talk to me."

"I bet he does."

"Don't you like to talk to me?"

"That's different."

"If it wasn't such a ridiculous idea, Doug, I'd think you were jealous of Alan Singer."

There was a pause, then, "Yeah, I guess you're right. And it is ridiculous, but there's nothing childlike about Alan."

"Why don't I just come by your place?"

"Because half the jocks in the school are always dropping by to see Woleski."

"Listen, I've got to finish reading this. We'll figure it out."

"I'll go work on the questionnaire."

"I'll see you in the morning."

She heard a chuckle. "You know what? This will be the first time I've looked forward to school since the first day I started teaching."

"I always look forward to your class."

"That's nice to know."

"Hey, Doug, if you were here now, would you kiss me good-night."

"Damn right."

"That's nice to know, too."

Chapter Eleven

*I'm in love. I really am. And he loves me, too. He
says I'm different from the other girls, more interesting. Since he told me that I try to think of ways
to be even more interesting. I'm so glad we moved
to Florida, although I'm sure fate would've found
a way for us to meet because we're perfect for each
other.*

JILL ENTERED CIVICS dressed in a short little skirt that
appeared to be the fashion in Palm Cove. He was early,
and she didn't even look over at his desk to see if he was
there already. He was trying not to stare at her, but he
couldn't stop his eyes from following her progress down
the aisle. The way her rear end moved beneath the skirt,
and then those slim legs beneath it—okay, so he
shouldn't be thinking those things. At least he wasn't
thinking them of a teenager.

He watched as she slid into the desk next to Alan's
and immediately leaned over and began whispering to
him. Alan started to smile, and Doug wished he knew
what she was saying. Then she suddenly straightened
around in her seat and saw him looking at her and he

quickly looked away. They couldn't smile at each other in class. No way could they do something like that.

The bell rang and Doug took roll. Then he got out the questionnaire he and Trader had stayed up late creating, and he had gone in early to run off this morning. As soon as he held them up, the class started to groan in unison. He was aware they thought it was a test, and he allowed them to suffer for a few moments.

"No, it's not a test," he finally said, but they didn't appear to be pacified. "Not even a quiz. This happens to be a sociological survey in dating patterns of high school students in South Florida."

That got a laugh for some reason.

"It's not a joke," he told them. "This is part of a project I'm working on, and I'm hoping to get my results published. Now you have every right to refuse to fill this out. If you don't want to help me out, you can study for one of your other classes while the rest do it. It's also confidential. You need not put your name on it, and I promise I won't grade you down for what you write. I won't grade you up, either. I hope you'll answer all questions honestly because the survey won't be valid if you don't. I want to thank you for your help in advance, and I'd appreciate your answering all questions fully."

"Is this about sex?" asked one of the boys.

"You'll find out in a minute," said Doug, sensing that even the word *sex* had perked up their interest.

He watched them for a few minutes as the surveys were passed out and some of the students flipped through the pages and read it first. He saw some smiles, saw some glances exchanged, and then most of them got to work on it.

Most of them finished before the class was over, but none of them brought their surveys up to his desk. At the end of the class they filed past his desk and placed them in a pile. He caught Jill's eye for a moment, and her look was mischievous. He immediately switched hers to the bottom of the pile.

During his junior civics class the next period, he gave them a quick test and read Jill's results. It wasn't any of his business; hers didn't even pertain to the subject, but he couldn't wait to see how she'd answered some of the questions. In fact—although he wouldn't have admitted this to her—he wrote some of the questions with her specifically in mind.

SOCIOLOGICAL SURVEY IN DATING PATTERNS OF HIGH SCHOOL STUDENTS IN SOUTH FLORIDA

Age __17__   Sex __F__

1. I started dating at age __12__

2. I have dated
    a) regularly __X__
    b) occasionally ____
    c) rarely ____
    d) never ____

3. I prefer to date
    a) someone older ____
    b) someone younger __X__
    c) someone my age ____

4. I like to date
    a) once a week ____
    b) more than once a week __X__

c) less than once a week ___
d) never ___

5. I am currently
   a) going steady ___
   b) dating different people ___
   c) dating one person but not going steady ___
   d) not dating but would like to _X_ *(soon!!)*
   e) not dating and don't want to ___

6. I date
   a) someone my parents approve of ___
   b) someone my friends like ___
   c) whomever I want to date _X_

7. My parents
   a) take an interest in whom I date ___
   b) don't care whom I date ___
   c) don't know whom I date _X_
   d) don't allow me to date ___

8. This school year I have so far dated _3_ different people.

9. I like to date for
   a) companionship ___
   b) popularity ___
   c) fun ___
   d) love ___
   e) other _____ sex _____

10. My favorite kind of date is
    a) movies ___
    b) sports event ___
    c) dance ___
    d) hanging out ___
    e) other ___ going to jungles ___

11. I have dated someone secretly
    a) once ____
    b) more than once _X_
    c) exclusively ____

12. I dated secretly because of
    a) parents' objection to person ____
    b) peer pressure ____
    c) dating partner's preference ____
    d) Intrigue _X_   *(oh, yes!)*

13. My dating experiences have been
    a) fantastic ____
    b) mostly good ____
    c) pretty good _X_   *(but could get better)*
    d) lousy ____
    e) nonexistent ____

14. I think it's okay for high school seniors to have sex if
    a) they love each other ____
    b) if they're going steady ____
    c) they both want to _X_
    d) they're married ____

15. I would date my friend's girlfriend/boyfriend
    a) if I felt like it ____
    b) if I didn't get caught ____
    c) never _X_

16. Please describe the best date you ever had.
    Well, it was in Central America, a war was going on not far from us, which added an element of excitement, and he was the most dangerous man I've ever known. He was as good-looking as Mel Gibson, as sexy as Kevin Costner, and I hadn't been alone with a man in

*months. He borrowed a Jeep and we headed out
of town. Soon we were at the jungle, but instead
of turning back, he parked the Jeep and we got
out. "Want to take a walk in there?" he asked
me. I was willing to take a walk anywhere with
him, so I said yes. The sun was getting ready to
set, it was ninety-five degrees in the shade with a
humidity to match, and I was willing to ignore
the insect population. He took my hand and we
pushed our way into the thick undergrowth,
coming at length to a clearing by a waterfall. The
waterfall looked too refreshing to resist, so
we.... I don't think you want to hear the rest of
this, Mr. Lacayo.*

He should've waited until after lunch to read it and
saved himself from certain indigestion.

A GROUP OF GIRLS walked by the table and she heard,
"Hi, Jill, hi, Phaedra."

"Hi," said Jill, but Phaedra looked too surprised to
speak.

"What was that all about?" Jill asked her.

"I think we're getting popular," said Phaedra.

"From what?"

"The dance, of course."

In last night's excitement, Jill had forgotten all about
the dance. "Why would the girls be speaking to us?"

"Because the boys are," said Phaedra. "A couple of
them said hello to me in the hall this morning, and the
girls noticed. If the boys like us, the girls figure they
better."

"Maybe one of us will be prom queen," joked Jill.

Phaedra shook her head. "That'll be Marla. Listen, where were you all day yesterday? I kept trying to call you."

"I met Alan and the guys at the beach."

"Was it fun?"

"No, it was creepy. The cops were all over the place because of that killing, and Alan showed me where that friend of yours drowned."

"You're getting a nice tan. I can't see where your sleeves ended anymore."

"How could someone drown off the end of that pier?" Jill asked her. "It isn't even that long."

"People drown in bathtubs," said Phaedra.

"I guess."

"So, did you have fun with Alan?"

"I told you; it was creepy."

"Wasn't the dance wonderful? My mother couldn't believe I had such a good time."

"Yeah, it was fun," said Jill.

"Everyone was talking about you dancing with Mr. Lacayo and embarrassing him."

Jill smiled. "He wouldn't even look at me in class this morning. He had some survey for us on dating habits of teenagers."

"You mean a test?"

"No. We didn't even put our names on them. He's doing some kind of research and wanted our help."

"Was it about sex and stuff like that?"

"Some of it," said Jill. "Like, would you date your friend's boyfriend, and would you date secretly so your parents wouldn't find out."

"What did you say?"

"I said I wouldn't date a friend's boyfriend and I would date secretly. It sounds like fun." She was hoping Phaedra would say her friend had dated secretly, but either she wasn't talking or Susan really had kept it a secret.

"No one could get away with dating secretly around here," said Phaedra.

"Why not?"

"It's too small a town."

"It's always possible," said Jill.

"I don't see how."

"You just meet the other person out of town, that's all."

"I'd rather date out in the open. Of course I guess I'd settle for secret if I really liked the boy."

"It sounds fun to me," said Jill.

"Listen, I'm signing up for a class in jazz dancing after school. You want to take it? It's only twenty dollars at the Parks Department."

"I don't have time," said Jill.

"It's only three hours a week and it's supposed to get you in good shape. I guess you're already in good shape, though."

"I really don't have the time," said Jill. "I have too much studying to do if I want to get good grades."

"Maybe you'd want to this summer."

"Maybe," said Jill. But not likely. She wondered what Phaedra was going to think when she suddenly disappeared from school. She guessed she owed it to her to call and explain, not that Phaedra was going to take the deception well.

"Hi, Jill, hi, Phaedra," said Mark, walking by the table on the way out of the cafeteria."

"He spoke to me," said Phaedra when he was out of sight.

"He thinks you're cute," said Jill.

"You're making that up."

"He danced with you, didn't he?"

Phaedra blushed pink from pleasure.

"CAN YOU BELIEVE THAT? Some remote jungle clearing with a waterfall?"

"Sounds pretty good to me," said Trader, reaching for the last piece of pizza.

"Better looking than Mel Gibson? How the hell do you compete with Mel Gibson?"

"Don't forget Kevin Costner," Trader reminded him.

"You think she's trying to tell me something?"

"I think she's pulling your leg, Lacayo."

"You really think so?"

"She's playing games with you. And why not? The survey wasn't intended for her."

"You think she just made it up?"

"Dougie, she's not seventeen. She's been around the block a few times, I imagine."

"What's that supposed to mean?"

"You know damn well what it means. What do you think, she's a twenty-seven-year-old virgin?"

"Of course not," said Doug, but he would like to think so.

"You haven't exactly been saving yourself for her for twenty-nine years."

"That's not the point."

"The point is, you're getting all bent out of shape for no reason."

"Do you really think she started dating at twelve?"

"That's the seventh grade. We were going to dances with girls in the seventh grade. We even took a few to the movies. And we were chasing them all over the place in the sixth grade, if you recall."

"Yeah, to wrestle with them."

"That was just our form of sex in those days, that's all. What did we know?"

"You're right, I'm overreacting. She did say she was not dating but would like to."

"You are going to date her, aren't you?"

"We'll have to sneak around, but yeah."

"I thought she lived alone?"

"She says Singer and his buddies stop by."

"Don't let them catch you there."

"I don't think they ought to be there. They're a little young to be hanging around her apartment."

"Yeah, but they don't know that. They think she's one of them."

"She acts like it. You ought to see her and Alan in class. They're always huddled together in the last row."

"Probably to make you jealous."

"You think so?"

Trader shrugged.

"Well, it's working."

"You're not jealous of Alan Singer."

"I guess not. She said she's dated three people this year."

"I imagine she had a social life before she came here."

"I haven't dated three people this year."

"You could've if you had wanted to."

"She thinks it's okay for high school students to have sex if they want to."

"So do I."

"I guess."

"You *guess*? Hell, don't you remember what it was like in high school? All we ever thought about was sex."

"I remember."

"Just thinking about it makes me feel old."

"Don't worry about it, Woleski, you haven't changed."

"You might not believe this, but I'm slowing down."

"I've come to a standstill."

"Yeah, but now you have Jill."

"Yeah."

"When are you going to see her?"

"I'm hoping tonight. We can go over the surveys."

"Right."

"Well, it won't take all that long."

"If you'd like me to vacate the premises, all you have to do is ask."

"And sixteen jocks would just happen to drop by."

"Yeah, I guess that wouldn't be smart."

"Anyway, it's too soon to be alone with her. I want to get to know her first."

"You got to know her last night."

"Yeah, but it's a school night."

"I don't get it, all that studying she does."

"I guess she doesn't want to look stupid in class."

"She was probably a real grind in college."

"I doubt it. She's just naturally bright."

"Are you thinking of running off to Africa with her when the school year is over?"

"And do what? Play Tarzan?"

"Maybe you could get a job like she has."

"Don't rush things."

"Me? You're beside yourself over her; I'm not the one rushing things."

"I really like her."

"No kidding. Next thing I know the two of you will be going steady."

JILL WALKED into study hall with Alan. He was telling her a joke, a stupid shaggy dog kind of story, but she loved stories like that and when he got to the punch line, she doubled over with laughter.

"I thought you'd like that."

"I've got to write that one down or I'll forget it," said Jill, taking out her notebook and writing just enough so that she'd remember the joke.

"Done your algebra homework?" he asked her.

"I did it in Spanish."

"Want me to check it for you?"

She handed it over, and he checked the answers against his own. "You don't need me anymore," he said.

"It's easy now that I remember it."

"Miss Wyckoff?" she heard and looked up at Doug's voice. He was motioning her to the front of the room.

"Maybe he wants to talk to you about your dating patterns," said Alan in a low voice.

"Not me, I disguised by handwriting," said Jill, going to the front of the room. With her back to the classroom, no one could see her, so she gave Doug a big smile.

He kept his face serious but she could tell it took an effort. "I was thinking," said Doug, keeping his voice pitched low.

"I think all the time," said Jill.

"Did anyone ever tell you you were a smartass?"

"Many times."

She could see him relax a little. "I thought we could go over those surveys tonight. I'm sure you're anxious to see them."

"Great idea."

"What about your place?"

She shook her head. "I told you, Alan and the guys stop by all the time. What about yours?"

"The same thing," he said.

She grinned at him. "Well, I guess we could go to a motel."

He practically turned white. "Keep your voice down," he whispered.

"No one heard that."

"I hope not."

"You're getting paranoid."

"Look, think about it, okay? I'll give you a call around six and we'll decide where to meet."

"I'll be counting off the minutes," said Jill.

"Stop that!"

"Really, Doug, you don't belong in teaching."

"Mr. Lacayo."

"I thought you said to call you Doug?"

"Not in school."

She shook her head. "I just hope you're a little more assertive tonight." She headed back to her desk without waiting for an answer. It was sure fun to make him squirm, but she didn't want to overdo it.

"What did he want?" asked Alan.

"He was supposed to inform me that my transcripts haven't arrived from Africa yet," she said, thinking fast.

"What did they do, send them by boat?"

As soon as Jill opened the door to her apartment, the phone started ringing. When she answered it, it was her mother.

"Honey? I'm here, visiting Carol. Why don't you come up to the house?"

"I'll be right there," said Jill.

Carol Wyckoff let her in the back door and led her through to a sun porch where the two women were having iced tea. "Can I get you anything?" asked Mrs. Wyckoff.

"I'd love a glass of that," said Jill, bending down to give her mother a kiss on the cheek.

"You're looking good," said her mother.

Jill told her about Doug.

"Well, I guess the poor man is relieved to find out you're an adult."

"Very relieved," said Jill. "He's helping me out, too," she said, then told both women about the survey.

"Your father and I have been talking about this, honey, and we really don't like you having to do this for us."

"I don't mind, Mom. I want to find out the truth, too."

"I've pretty much come to believe you're right. If Susan didn't sound suicidal in her diary, and she certainly seemed happy at home, then it must have been a freak accident of some kind. And much as we love having you nearby, your dad and I think we're being very selfish keeping you from your work. We're very proud of what you're doing over there."

"I'd like to give it a few more weeks," said Jill, "and see if I come up with anything. Anyway, if you make me go back now, you'll be depriving me of all the good junk food over here."

"Did I hear a man being mentioned when I was in the kitchen?" asked Carol Wyckoff.

Jill's mom nodded. "I think that's what's really keeping her here."

"No it's not," said Jill, "but it has made it more interesting."

"I don't know if it's smart you getting involved with someone," said her mother. "It's not going to be easy to leave him."

"Who's leaving him?" asked Jill.

"You're going to stay here?"

Her mother looked so happy she hated to disappoint her. "No, Mom, but I'm going to try to talk him into coming over. He doesn't like teaching here, and we could really use him in Ethiopia."

"Does he know about this?"

Jill grinned. "Not yet."

"I assume you're just seeing him in school."

"I'm seeing him tonight," said Jill, "if he can come up with a safe place. I suppose we'll have to meet out of town."

"Someone's bound to see you one of these times," said her mother.

"Not if we disguise her as an adult," said Carol. "Although I must say I'm jealous of the way you look in that miniskirt."

"I'm a little shocked," said her mother. "I thought you didn't go in for skirts. I could never get you out of your jeans."

"It's cooler," said Jill.

"Isn't it funny," said Carol, "how women with good legs always claim miniskirts are cooler. You never hear women with fat legs making that claim."

"In Ethiopia I wear these long, white cotton dresses that all the women there wear, and they really are cooler. The point is to keep as much sun off your body as possible."

"A little makeup," said Carol, "maybe a dress and heels. I even have a wig you can wear."

Jill started to laugh.

"Listen to her," said her mother. "You don't want to get him fired, do you?"

"You just want to see me transformed, Mom."

"Well, I don't know why you had to cut your hair off like a boy."

"Because it's easier to get the lice out."

"She thinks she's shocking me," her mom said to Carol, "but I've seen worse things than lice."

Carol smiled. "Let's take her upstairs, Jean, and play Barbie Doll with her."

"I never liked dolls when I was a child," said her mother.

"Neither did I," said Carol, "but this could be fun."

Jill groaned. "Why do I get the feeling I'm being manipulated?"

Chapter Twelve

Doug walked into the restaurant expecting to see Jill, since he had spotted her car in the parking lot. She wasn't hanging around the entrance, though, and the hostess hadn't seen her. He peered into the bar, didn't spot her and stood at the end of the bar where he could keep an eye out for her. He ordered a beer from the bartender.

He was a little nervous. This wasn't exactly a date, but it was pretty close to one, and he wanted to make a good impression. It was bad enough having his date meet him thirty miles to the north of Palm Cove and insisting they take separate cars. He wanted the dinner to go just right, the two of them all alone.... He was sure that had been her car he'd seen in the parking lot.

He spotted the door to the ladies' room off to his left and decided that was where she was. He'd just keep an eye on the door; she shouldn't be much longer.

Out of the corner of his eye he noticed a frosted blonde in a fancy pink dress and long, silky legs in matching heels. The frosted hair was a giveaway that she was an older woman and not a natural blonde. A lot of his mother's friends back in Chicago got their hair frosted that color the first time they spotted a gray hair. Not that he was interested; it was just an observation.

He sensed her watching him and had a feeling she was on the prowl. Trying not to be obvious about it, he moved a little away from her at the bar.

"Buy me a drink, handsome?" a low, husky voice with a Southern drawl was asking.

Doug pretended to be both hard of hearing and invisible. The last thing he wanted was for Jill to come out of the bathroom and see him talking to another woman. And this one sounded as though she was apt to do more than just talk, even in a bar.

The voice became teasing. "I'm talking to you, good-looking."

Doug considered leaving the restaurant and waiting out in the parking lot. Only, if Jill was in the ladies' room, she wouldn't be looking for him in the parking lot. He could stand outside the door to the bathroom but that would look suspect.

He heard a rather theatrical sigh. "Whenever I see a man with Mel Gibson's looks and Kevin Costner's sex appeal, I immediately think of bolting for the jungle."

The words penetrated, and he made the connection to the words on the survey, but he still had to do a double take and even then it still didn't make sense. And yet... "Jill?" he asked, very uncertain.

"Glad you finally recognized me," she said, and now he recognized the voice.

"But you look so...so...mature."

"I decided to dispense with the Lolita look for the evening."

"No one would recognize you."

"That's the point, Mr. Lacayo."

And now it was the smartass voice she used in class, but it seemed peculiar coming out of that bright pink mouth, the face surrounded by masses of stiff-looking hair.

He leaned in closer for a better look. "Are those your own eyelashes?"

"Actually they belong to Mrs. Wyckoff."

"The hair—"

"A wig."

He shook his head a little. "I feel like I'm out with my mother."

"No, Doug—be honest. You feel like you're being picked up by an older woman on the make." She got up and slipped her arm through his. "And everyone at the bar thinks you are." She leaned into him so that her stiff hair tickled his chin.

He looked around and saw several men eyeing them. What the hell, they were probably envious. She was the best looking woman at the bar, even if she was the only one.

"It's all that makeup," he tried to explain. "It ages you."

"Just be glad I didn't waltz in here looking fourteen."

"You look kind of...glamorous."

"Tacky is the word, Doug—don't be afraid to use it. I got carried away with the disguise. Listen, I was embarrassed just walking in here like this."

"The dress is nice."

"Maybe for the mother of the bride at an afternoon wedding."

He took a closer look at the dress and noticed the lace and all the tiny pink beads sewn onto it. She was right. He remembered seeing older women wearing dresses just like it at weddings in Chicago. "It seems funny seeing you dressed up. If I'd known, I would've put on a jacket."

"One of us might as well look normal," she said. "Are we going to eat or what? I'm starving."

IF SHE LOOKED past Doug, Jill could see a view of the water. It was still light out and sailboats and cabin cruisers and motor boats pulling water skiers kept going by, diverting her attention from the menu. She still couldn't get over the fact that everywhere she drove in south Florida there was so much water.

"They have good steaks," said Doug, bringing her attention back to the menu. "I'm going to get a sirloin."

"I think I'll have fish," she said, unobtrusively removing Mrs. Wyckoff's uncomfortable shoes beneath the table.

"The fish is good, too."

Jill caught sight of a word she hadn't expected to see. "Dolphin? Isn't it against the law to eat dolphins?"

"That's not the kind that talk. These are much smaller, just regular fish."

"Have you ever eaten it?"

"Sure. Order it, I think you'll like it. Listen, order anything you want."

"I will, since I plan on paying for it," said Jill.

"No."

"Yes."

"I want this to be on me," said Doug.

"It's not like this is a date."

"I feel like it's a date. I'd like it to be a date."

Jill started to smile. "Okay. I guess I'd like it to be a date, too." God knows, she'd fantasized about going out with him often enough.

"Who ever would've thought a week ago..."

"I would've. But then I knew I wasn't seventeen a week ago," she said.

"I wish I'd known."

The waiter brought a basket of freshly baked bread and took their order. "You want to share a bottle of wine?" Doug asked her.

"I don't know. We've got work to do, don't we?"

"I can drink wine and work," he said.

"Okay. I guess I can, too." She looked past him out the window and saw a brightly colored parachute going by over a boat. "Oh, look."

Doug turned around. "Parasailing. You ever been?"

"I've never even seen it."

"Maybe we can go sometime. If you're here long enough."

"I think I'll stay for the summer," said Jill, "visit with my parents."

He looked relieved at that. He must have thought she'd be leaving immediately.

He looked as if he wanted to say something, but it wasn't until their salads arrived that he asked, "You really started dating at twelve?"

Jill thought back to some of the silly answers she had filled out on the form. "I lied."

"Oh," he said, sounding pleased.

"I thought it sounded better."

"How old were you when you started dating?"

"Ten."

"Ten?"

"I went to the movies with Kenny Fitz in the fifth grade, and he used to chase me home after school and push me in the bushes."

"He pushed you in the bushes?"

"It was his way of saying he was interested. I did worse to him, though. I used to grab his homework in the schoolyard before school and tear it up."

"And that was your way of saying you were interested?"

"No, that was my way of getting even."

Doug shrugged. "It's none of my business, anyway. I mean, that questionnaire wasn't aimed at you."

The waiter poured some wine for Doug's approval. "Fine," said Doug, and both glasses were filled.

Jill took a sip of the wine and didn't think it was so fine, but he probably knew more about wine than she did. About all she ever drank was beer.

"How old were you when you started dating, Doug?"

"Seventh grade, I guess. There were Friday-night dances at the 'Y.'"

"We had those, too."

"Did the girls mostly dance with the girls?"

She nodded. "At your 'Y,' too?"

"Yeah. Most of the guys didn't know how to dance." He seemed to concentrate on his salad for a minute, separating the tomatoes and cucumbers from the lettuce, and then eating only the lettuce. She thought the two of them could save a lot of money on salads as she never ate the lettuce.

When the lettuce had disappeared from his bowl, he looked up at her and asked, "What were you like when you were a kid?"

She had never had a man ask her that before. She didn't think any of the men she had known cared what she was like when she was a kid. She thought back and came up with her most powerful memory. "Well, before I got interested in boys, I was obsessed with flying."

"You wanted to be a pilot?"

She shook her head. "I'm not talking about planes. *I* wanted to fly."

"What do we have here, Peter Pan?"

"I don't think I knew about Peter Pan when it started. I used to take books out of the library on birds. I was convinced if I found the right one it would give the secret of flying. Did you ever jump off the roof when you were a kid?"

Doug laughed. "I lived in Chicago, in a six-story building. I wouldn't be here now if I'd tried that."

"I used to jump off the garage roof into the backyard. I'd get all the kids in the neighborhood to do it. I really believed if I kept trying it would work some day. I can remember one whole year when I ate very little in order to get down to the right weight to fly."

"You ever try hang gliding?"

"No. I finally gave it up. Sometimes, though, I dream I can fly. It's wonderful, the most powerful feeling."

"Do you like flying in jets?"

"No, that's not flying. That's just sitting there being bored while the plane flies. Didn't you ever want to fly?"

"I don't remember ever wanting to fly. I can remember wanting to be invisible."

"Everyone fantasizes about that," she said.

Doug said, "I used to collect stamps."

"Stamps?"

"What can I tell you, I was a boring kid."

"I imagine stamp collecting could be interesting."

"I can still remember the stamps from Ethiopia. When you first said you were from there, it reminded me of them. They were pretty stamps."

"I'll send you some."

"I don't even know what happened to my stamp collection. My mother probably has it put away somewhere. I had to collect something; all my friends collected baseball cards."

"I collected baseball cards. I cornered the market on Juan Marachal and then refused to trade him. Were you a Cub fan?"

"White Sox," said Doug. "That thing you wrote," he began, then changed his mind when the waiter came to take away their salad bowls.

"What thing?"

"Nothing."

"No, what?"

He picked up a piece of bread and avoided her eyes. "About being in the jungle."

She grinned. "Did it whet your interest?"

"No, I didn't mean anything like that."

"It was supposed to."

"It was?"

"I was flirting with you, Mr. Lacayo."

He was smiling now. "You were? You mean you just made it up to get a rise out of me?"

"Oh, no—it was true."

"Oh."

"Hey, I'm not seventeen. I was involved with a guy when I was in the Peace Corps."

"You involved now?"

"No."

"No boyfriend?"

"No. What about you?"

"I was pretty serious about a woman in Chicago, but she got transferred to Houston and we broke up."

"No one in Miami?"

"No. Well . . ."

"Yes?"

"I feel like I'm starting to get involved with you."

Over their main course he questioned her about the Peace Corps and her work in Ethiopia. He seemed really interested, not as though he was just being polite, so she told him about it in some detail. She hoped she was whetting his appetite with this, too, as she had every intention of trying to talk him into going back to Ethiopia with her. That is, if things worked out. As far as she could see, though, they were.

He was really easy to be with and after a while she figured out why. He didn't treat her like a child or a mental defective or a helpless little woman or any of the other methods of treatment she had come to expect from men. He didn't pull age on her or education or experience or anything else. Come to think of it, he didn't with his students, either. He just generally treated people with respect, and she liked that.

"I like the dolphin," she said, "but I wish they'd call it something else."

"They're just regular little fish with no intelligence. Trader and I have caught a few."

"You go fishing?"

"Once in a while. Trader likes to go fishing off the Keys."

"I hear it's great down there."

"You want to drive down some time?"

"I'd love to."

"How about this weekend?"

"No, but I'll tell you what, Doug. As soon as I've found out what happened to Susan, we'll go down the very next weekend. If you still want to."

"I'm sorry. I completely forgot why we were here tonight."

She reached out and put her hand on top of his. "That's okay, I did, too."

He turned his hand over and clasped hers. "You know, ever since you told me about her, I've been trying to remember her. The thing is, she was quiet. She never volunteered in class. Not that most of them do."

"Can you picture her?"

"I'm not sure. If she looked like you, then I don't think so."

"She had a rounder face and a lot more hair."

"That's half the girls in the school."

"Do you remember who she sat next to?"

He nodded. "I remember that because I read about her death in the paper and then there was this empty desk the next day. She sat in the second row, the third seat in from the window."

"Who sat next to her?"

"Girls. If you're thinking she sat next to the prince, she didn't. You're the only student I've had who breezes in and sits with the boys. I noticed you right away."

"I was trying to be noticed."

"Trader thought you had guts."

"What did you think?"

"I attributed it to being the child of missionaries and not knowing any better. You want dessert?"

"I don't think so. Just coffee."

As their table was being cleared off, Doug reached down and took a bunch of papers out of his backpack.

"I separated the boys from the girls. We'll be able to verify their handwriting, too, against some papers I brought."

"Let's separate them by who dated secretly and who didn't," said Jill.

"They could lie about it."

"Sure, but why would they?"

"I guess we could eliminate the ones who go steady, too."

She shook her head. "A good reason for dating secretly would be because you're going steady."

"You really think kids are that devious?"

"Sure they are," Jill assured him. "Sexual attraction can make you do all sorts of devious things."

"Like walking into the laundromat with a copy of *Lolita* under your arm?"

"Exactly. But that wasn't intentional."

"Asking me to dance was."

"Oh, absolutely. I was out to get you that night."

"I know."

Jill looked through her questionnaires. Out of seven boys, two admitted to dating secretly. Neither was going steady.

"How many have you got?" she asked him.

"One, and he's going steady."

"I've got two and one of them's Alan."

"How do you know?"

"I recognize his handwriting."

"From all the notes he writes you?" He sounded annoyed as though she shouldn't exchange notes in class with Alan.

"Let's compare the handwriting," she said, wanting to get off the subject of Alan.

Doug reached into his bag again. "I've got a set of quizzes here, just the boys." He handed a bunch to Jill.

"You didn't grade them."

"What's the point? You were the only one who passed."

"Am I your star pupil?"

"You could say that."

"Are you going to give me an A?"

"I can't believe how serious you sound. Do you really care what grade I give you?"

"Yes."

"You probably won't even be there when report cards come out."

"I'd still like to know."

"Grading you would create a problem, you know. Next to you, everyone in there looks stupid."

"They're not stupid. They just don't read the paper."

"Yes, but in civics that's all they're required to do."

She started comparing the boys' handwriting to the quiz papers and she pretty quickly came up with a name. "I should've known," she said.

"What's that?"

"It's Peter. I already figured him for a potential prince when I asked him out."

"You did *what*?"

"I asked him out on a date. We went to the movies."

"And was he a prince?" asked Doug, an unexpected touch of sarcasm in his voice.

"Hardly. He was a handful. But I questioned him quite a bit and I'd swear he wasn't the prince."

"Here it is," said Doug, putting a quiz by the side of a questionnaire. "It's Judd Winston. He goes steady with one of the cheerleaders; I think her name is Cindi."

"I can't picture him," said Jill.

"You should be able to; he sits in your row."

"Which side of me?"

"Next to the window."

She still couldn't form a picture of him. "Dark hair?"

Doug nodded.

"What's he like?"

"Pretty good halfback."

"So how do I get him to go out with me when he's going steady with a cheerleader?"

"Maybe it's time to put the fear of God into them."

"Meaning what?"

"Get them alone, one by one, and lie. Say your sister wrote all about the prince in her diary, even his name."

"That'll blow my cover."

"It's not doing you any good, anyway."

"I have a feeling it's Judd," said Jill.

"I have a feeling it's Alan."

Something in his tone made her look up. "You really don't like him, do you?"

"I think he's pretty arrogant, that's all."

"Sure he's arrogant; he's a genius."

"Did he tell you that?"

"Yes."

"That's what I mean."

"I like him."

"I know you do."

"Don't tell me you're jealous of a kid."

He looked bemused. "Intellectually, no, but when I see the two of you together, I don't know."

"If it weren't for Alan, I'd be flunking algebra."

"What difference would it make? You don't have to pass algebra."

"I enjoy his company. He seems older."

"Yeah, he does seem older," said Doug. "He doesn't seem like a kid when I coach him, either. Not that he pays any attention to me."

Jill said, "I really think it's Judd. Say he was seeing Susan on the sly, they're fooling around on the pier one night and an accident happens.... He'd be scared to say anything for fear Cindi would find out. That's the way kids think, you know. It makes sense."

"When are you going to confront them?"

"I'll do it tomorrow night, and all in the same night before word gets around. I call them all and say I have to talk to them." She grinned. "If I'm lucky, I'll only have one more day of school."

"And we won't have to sneak around anymore."

"Peter and Alan will be easy, but if Judd gives me a hard time, I'll just show up at his house."

"I'll go with you."

"Would you?"

"Sure."

Jill reached out a foot and rubbed it against his ankle.

Doug captured her foot between his ankles. "I think I caught myself something."

"I believe you did."

"Should I reel it in or throw it back?"

"Couldn't we go somewhere more private to do this? It's kind of distracting being in a restaurant."

"The only thing in here distracting is you," he said, but he didn't let go of her foot.

"You're pretty distracting yourself, Mr. Lacayo. Do you know I used to daydream about you in class?"

"You didn't have time. You were always arguing with me in class."

"I used to write your name in my notebook in study hall."

"You used to write notes to Alan Singer in study hall."

"When I followed you home and saw that big house, I figured at first you were married."

"Did you mind?"

She nodded.

"I wouldn't have gotten married before I met you."

Jill could feel the smile taking over her face. "That's the nicest thing anyone ever said to me."

"Your being twenty-seven is the nicest thing that's ever happened to me."

"Let's go out to your car and fool around," she said, unable to stop the enthusiasm from showing in her voice.

Her foot dropped to the floor as Doug looked around to see if she had been overheard.

"You don't have to look so shocked," she said. "Ever since I've been back in high school I've felt like making out in a car. I guess it's nostalgia."

"It sounds like you already have been. I didn't know you'd been dating the boys."

"Only Peter that one time and all I did with him was fight him off in the car. And he was worse in the movies."

"I don't want to hear about it."

"Good, because I'm getting tired of talking. Let's get out of here."

"I feel like I'm taking advantage of you."

"I'm not seventeen."

"I know you're not. You don't even look it. But some part of me still thinks of me as the teacher and you as the student."

"You'll get over it."

Doug smiled as he signaled the waiter for their check.

"WHAT ARE YOU DOING?" he asked her when they got to the parking lot and she headed for her car.

"I just have to get something," she said, going over to her car and opening it. She reached in and brought out a canvas satchel.

Doug couldn't believe his eyes. "What're you doing with an overnight bag?"

"It's not an overnight bag. What do you think I did, pack an overnight bag in case we ended up at a motel?"

He was thinking exactly that, and he was both shocked and titillated by the prospect. "What's in it?"

She placed the bag on his fender and unzipped it. "Just take a look, please, and calm down."

"I don't think I want to see."

"It's your laundry—freshly washed and dried. If you don't want it back, I'll continue wearing it."

"I feel really stupid," he said, which was putting it mildly.

"You should." But instead of acting angry, she moved up against him and put her arms around him.

He pulled her closer to him and leaned down to kiss her. Despite the fact that her dress felt stiff and her hair was scratchy and he ordinarily hated the touch of thick lipstick against his mouth, there was something altogether right and wonderful about the kiss, and he supposed it was because he was kissing Jill.

When he finally came up for air, she said, "Come on, let's get in the back seat."

"I don't think this is such a good idea," said Doug, looking around. "There are too many people here. Someone's bound to see us."

"They won't know who it is."

"Our cars are pretty recognizable."

"You're really paranoid, aren't you?"

"I'm sorry, I guess I am."

She grinned at him. "If you get in the back seat with me, I'll take off my wig."

"I have a better idea. Let's go to a motel."

"Why, Mr. Lacayo, I don't believe what I'm hearing. Only a moment ago you almost fainted when I mentioned the word motel."

"You're the one who's supposed to act shocked at the idea."

"Just think of me as an older woman out to seduce a young jock."

"Not so young."

"We'll call it youngish."

He opened the door for her, and she threw the bag in the back before climbing in.

HE LEFT HER in the car and went into the lobby, only to turn around and go right back out. He couldn't believe his bad luck. Out of all the motels within forty miles of Palm Cove, he had to pick the one where Harvey Gold of the Palm Cove School Board just happened to be checking in with a woman young enough to be his daughter.

Jill started to get out of the car and he yelled out, "Get back in; we're leaving."

"If you're afraid to do it, I'll do the checking in," she said, all the way out of the car now.

"Get in and I'll explain," he said, opening the door to his side and almost throwing himself in.

She took the seat beside him with great reluctance. "If you're nervous about it, I guess we shouldn't do it."

"I'm not that nervous. It's just that one of the members of the school board is in there checking in."

"Did he see you?"

"I don't think so."

"Was he with his wife?"

"It sure didn't look like it. Anyway, why would he be going to a motel with his wife?"

"I don't know why he scared you off, then. You're a single teacher; you're entitled to be here. He's the one who's committing adultery."

"He won't see it that way. He'll just see me as a threat to his reputation and get me fired."

"He wouldn't dare."

"Look, I don't want to argue about it. There's got to be other motels around here."

"Is that him coming out?"

"Don't look!"

"He can't see me, Doug. Look, they're getting into a car. They're leaving. He must've been checking out."

Doug sneaked a look around and saw the car pull out of the parking lot.

"Do you want me to go in?"

"Maybe we should just make out a little in the car."

"Well, that's tempting," said Jill, "but it seems really silly to make out in a car in a motel parking lot."

"This is going to sound stupid, but I feel like I'm breaking some law."

"I'll check in."

"No, I'll do it."

"I'll come with you."

"No!"

"You know what? I think you're embarrassed to be seen with me because I'm dressed like your mother."

"You do look a little flashy," he said.

"Am I hearing you right? The sexy Mr. Lacayo is actually something of a prude?"

"I'm just nervous."

"I make you nervous?"

"Hell yes! You've made me nervous for weeks."

"I'm going to make you more nervous if you don't go check us in. You've got ten seconds, then I'm going to put on your underwear and parade around the parking lot in it."

Doug was out of the car in two seconds flat.

HE WATCHED HER as she looked at herself in the mirror and grimaced. "I'm going to go wash some of this makeup off," she said, disappearing into the bathroom.

He looked around. It was a pretty nice motel, a lot neater than his house. There were two double beds, a cable TV, a table and two chairs and even a small refrigerator. He wouldn't mind living in it, and it was right on the beach.

He heard water running in the bathroom and decided to get out of his clothes before she came out. Getting out of clothes was always awkward, and he could save them from that. She was probably doing the same thing in there.

He undressed in a hurry, then pulled the bedspread off one of the beds and got under the covers. He couldn't remember ever being this excited about a woman. Well, maybe the first time he was, but then it was mostly nerves. Claire had never really excited him, which was probably why he hadn't minded when she told him she was being transferred. And since then he hadn't been interested in anybody. Until now. And this time he was very interested. In fact it wasn't going to take much to admit to having fallen hard.

He reached over and turned off the bedside lamp so that only the lamp on the dresser was lit. It was still kind of bright, but he wanted to see her. He was just starting to imagine her opening the bathroom door and walking out naked, when the bathroom door opened and she came out fully dressed.

"I feel pretty stupid," he groaned.

"Why?" she asked, her face looking fresh without makeup.

"I guess I was rushing things."

"Not at all," she said. "But I wanted to treat you to the transformation of the older woman to the real me."

"Do you need some music for this?"

"This is a transformation, not a strip, but you can hum if you want."

She reached up and pulled something off her eyelids, then handed it to him. He looked down at his hand and the false eyelashes looked like two black insects with lots of legs. He transferred them to the clean ashtray on the table.

"Are you ready?" she asked him.

"I'm ready."

She pulled off the wig and she started to look like herself again. Her hair was kind of mashed flat, but she fluffed it up with her fingers and grinned her familiar grin. "Any improvement yet?"

"Absolutely."

She walked over to the bed and turned so that her back was to him. "Unzip me, please."

His hand was sweating as he pulled down the zipper, causing it to catch once in his eagerness.

She stepped back from the bed and pulled the dress over her head. Beneath it she was wearing a lacy slip. It had been a long time since he had seen a woman in a slip.

"Did you ever see a slip before?" she asked him.

"Well . . ."

"Take a good look because you'll never see me in one again."

He thought she was going to take the slip off then, but instead she reached up beneath it and somehow managed to get her pantyhose off without revealing anything.

"Okay, get ready for the real me," she said, and despite her bravado, he could tell she was just as nervous as he was.

She lifted the slip over her head, let it drop to the floor, and then she was standing there in white cotton pants and nothing else and he didn't think he'd ever seen anyone more beautiful in his life.

"Well, Mr. Lacayo?"

Doug threw aside the covers and beckoned her. "Get into this bed at once, Ms. Wyckoff, and let's see about improving your grade."

Chapter Thirteen

"You got in late last night," observed Trader, pouring Doug a mug of coffee.

"Yeah," agreed Doug.

"You were with Jill?"

"Uh-huh."

"Verbose this morning, aren't we?"

"Give me a break, Woleski; my eyes are barely open."

"I would think so after—what was it, three hours' sleep?"

"What're you, my mother?"

"So how'd it go? You figure out who the prince was?"

"It was a lot of work," said Doug. "First we had to check out the questionnaires, then we had to do handwriting comparisons—"

"Oh, right. That took you until four in the morning."

"We ate dinner first."

"Don't ever try to put something over on someone, Lacayo, because your face is an open book."

"Yeah? And what are you reading?"

"You look awfully happy for someone who only got three hours' sleep and is going to a job he hates."

"Can I help it if I'm in a good mood?"

"So what else happened last night?"

"We had a good time together, okay?"

"I don't know, you're acting different somehow."

"You want to know the truth, Woleski? I'm in love. Okay?"

"In other words, mind my own business."

"No, I'm serious—I'm in love."

"Yeah, right, and I'm the coach of the Dolphins."

JILL FELT LIKE playing hookey from school and calling up Doug to see if he wanted to play hookey with her. She just couldn't go to school and show up in his class as if nothing had happened. She'd never be able to pull it off. Just her face smiling back at her in the mirror was enough to make her suspicious. She never smiled this early in the morning. And if she could see it, everyone else would be able to see it, too.

She felt like calling up her mother and telling her she was in love. Only it didn't seem right her being in love, not when it never would've happened if it hadn't been for Susan. She felt a twinge of guilt for her happiness, but only a twinge as she was feeling so damn happy nothing could bring her down from the high she was on.

She'd have to remember to drop Mrs. Wyckoff's dress off at the cleaners. Ugly as it was, she now loved that dress. It was her lucky dress. She wondered what Doug would do if she walked into class wearing it. She knew what the kids would do; they would roar with laughter. Poor Doug would probably collapse behind his desk. Not that it was going to be much easier walking in there in her regular clothes.

She should be exhausted after only three hours' sleep but she felt energized. She hadn't even wanted that sleep; only Doug had insisted. He said he was afraid if he spent even one more minute with her, he was in danger of running off with her and never going back to school again. She had been tempted to take him up on it. Well, she'd get him to run away with her, but it would be after the school year and directly to Ethiopia. Which she would just happen to suggest to him the next time they were alone together. Last night in the motel had been relatively free of discussions of any sort.

She picked up her books and was out the door before she remembered she hadn't done her algebra homework. For a moment she panicked, then reason took over. So what could Mr. Colwin do, flunk her? Did it really matter? The only thing that mattered now was finding out who the prince was so that she and Doug could get on with their lives.

JILL WALKED into civics, slid her eyes over to Doug's desk and watched him quickly look away. He had a smile on his face, though, that he couldn't conceal.

"Good morning, Mr. Lacayo," she said, projecting just the right tone of youth and innocence.

She saw the muscles in his back tense up, then he looked around, as though just spotting her. "Oh, good morning, Jill," he said, before quickly looking down at some papers on his desk.

Jill slid into the desk next to Alan and got out her notebook. Almost immediately a note was passed to her.

"Did you and Lacayo have a good time?"

Jill froze in space for a fraction of a second, then turned her reaction to one of bewilderment.

"What're you talking about?" she said to him in a normal tone of voice.

He gave her the kind of condescending look a cat gives to a mouse right before it pounces. "Where were you last night?"

"I had dinner with my aunt and uncle."

"Really?"

"What're you doing, Alan, spying on me?"

"If I spied on you, would I see you and Lacayo together?"

"I don't know why you came up with this, but I wish you'd just drop it. I don't mind you thinking it about me, but you could get Lacayo fired."

"Did I say anything? Just having some fun with you, Jilly. Anyway, I can relate. I've been attracted to older women."

"Anyway, he's not my type," said Jill.

"Who's your type?"

"Mel Gibson."

Alan shook his head and looked disappointed. "I would've expected you to be more original than that."

"His appeal is universal," said Jill, then quit talking when Doug stood up and asked for quiet.

And for the rest of the class it was all she could do to tear her eyes away from him.

LIKE THE VERY WORST KIND of love-struck adolescent, Jill found herself bringing Doug into the conversation at lunch, just to be able to speak his name aloud. Not that she called him Doug. What she said was, "Mr. Lacayo's doing a survey of teenage dating habits."

"I heard," said Phaedra, not sounding particularly interested.

"What did you hear?"

"Some of the girls were talking about it, that's all."

"He couldn't be that old," said Jill. "He must know all about teenage dating."

Phaedra stopped chewing long enough to say, "A lot of the teenage girls in this school would like to hear about his dating habits."

"Really?" asked Jill, trying to sound as if the thought had never occurred to her.

"A lot of the girls have crushes on him."

"Well, he's pretty good-looking," said Jill, thinking that saying anything else would be unbelievable.

"He's *great* looking."

"I guess. Do you have a crush on him, Phaedra?"

"Sure. Who doesn't?"

"I don't."

"I don't know about you, Jill. You don't go for Alan, you don't go for Lacayo... Jack must really be something."

It took her a moment to remember who Jack was. "He is. Tall, blond, very sweet. He's British."

"Sounds boring to me," said Phaedra.

It sounded boring to Jill, too. "Well, there weren't many boys our age over there."

"You know who really had a crush on Lacayo?" asked Phaedra, a secretive smile on her face.

"Who?" asked Jill, about a million light years away from being prepared for the answer.

"My friend," said Phaedra, looking straight into Jill's eyes. "The one who killed herself."

Something fully alive only moments before seemed to die in Jill.

Phaedra gave her a knowing look. "She always called him 'the prince,' but I knew who she was talking about."

SPANISH WAS a nightmare. While the rest of the class took a test, Jill sat in a stupor, not even able to lift her pencil.

Everything fit: the prince in civics, the reason for keeping it secret, his reason to maintain silence after the act. What's more, if Doug was the prince, it could've been a suicide. He could even have killed her to shut her up.

No, he couldn't be the prince. It wasn't possible that knowing she was Susan's sister, he then could've made love to her, told her he loved her. Only a monster would behave like that, and Doug wasn't a monster.

But what if he was? What if she was letting her attraction for him cloud her judgment? Wasn't it always the ones closest to murderers who claimed their innocence, who said their son or their brother or their husband couldn't do a thing like that? Wasn't love blind?

And, despite her trying to prevent the thought from surfacing, still it came up: if he was the prince, the hardest thing to live with was the fact she'd be forever jealous of her dead sister. She had never known how strong guilt could be until that moment. How it could make her literally sick, so that she had to excuse herself to Ms. Lopez and flee to the girls' room.

She threw up her lunch into the toilet bowl, then splashed cold water on her face. She had to get out of here. She had to go home.

She waited for the bell to ring, then lost herself in the crowded halls until she was by the front door and then out in the parking lot. She had to get out of there. She had to be alone.

But what was she going to do? *What in the name of God was she going to do?*

SHE DROVE AROUND for hours, trying to lose herself in the driving, but it didn't work. When she finally got home, the phone rang. Afraid it was Doug, she hesitated in picking it up. When she finally answered after the twenty-seventh ring, it was Alan.

"Oh, hi," she said, relieved it was he.

"Took you long enough to answer."

"I just walked in."

"Where'd you disappear to?"

"I cut out in Spanish and didn't go back."

"I admire your guts."

"It wasn't guts. I wasn't feeling so hot; I think it was something I ate."

"That cafeteria food'll do it to you every time. Listen, Jill, about last night . . ."

"What about it? I told you I was eating with my aunt and uncle."

"It won't wash."

"What do you care what I was doing last night, Alan?"

"Well, I just happened to be driving by your house, and I just happened to see this blonde in a pink dress getting into your car . . . so I followed her."

Jill's first instinct was to hang up, but instead she hung in there. "Alan, I don't know what—"

"Jill, I need to talk to you."

"I'm sorry, Alan, but I don't feel like talking."

"Not on the phone. In person."

"Whatever you're thinking, Alan—"

"Don't hang up!"

"I wasn't going to hang up."

"I feel like we're friends, Jill, and as a friend, there's something I think you should know about Lacayo."

It was so quiet she could hear his breath.

"Are you there?" he asked.

"I'm here."

"How about meeting me down by the pier?"

"Can't you just tell me whatever it is over the phone?"

"I'd rather tell you in person. Anyway, I think you might need a friend around."

"I don't know, Alan."

"Please? In about a half hour? Before the sun sets?"

"All right."

"You'll be there?"

"I'll be there."

When the phone rang again almost as soon as she hung up, she thought it was Alan calling back and picked it up.

"What?" she answered.

"*What?* Is that any way to answer a phone?"

It was Doug and she didn't know what to say.

"Hey, Jill, you okay? Where were you in study hall?"

She had to be calm. She couldn't let him know her suspicions. "I wasn't feeling so well after lunch so I came home."

"I tried to get you earlier."

"I unplugged my phone and took a nap."

She heard his chuckle. "Yeah, I'm suffering from a little lack of sleep today, too."

The memory of making love to him the night before created havoc with her nerves. "Look, Doug, I can't talk right now."

"I thought maybe you'd like to meet somewhere—"

"Not tonight," she said. "I have to go." Then she hung up the phone before unplugging it. So what if he wondered why she hung up on him? If he was the prince, she didn't give a damn what he wondered. And if he wasn't, well, she'd take care of that later.

"SHE HUNG UP on me."

"One party in a telephone conversation usually hangs up first," said Trader.

"She didn't even say good-bye."

"Probably the morning-after jitters."

"But she was fine this morning. Why would she hang up on me tonight?"

"Relax and watch the ball game."

Doug picked up the phone and dialed her number again. He let it ring twenty times before giving up. "Now she's not answering the phone."

"Will you quit it, Lacayo? You're acting like a teenager."

"I'm worried about her."

"What's to worry about?"

"I don't know, but I think something's wrong."

"Look, Lacayo, if I know women—and I *do* know them—sometimes they just want to be left alone."

"I'm going over there."

"As soon as you do that, someone's going to spot you."

"I don't care."

Trader got up and took him by the arm, marched him over to the couch and shoved him down. "Now what exactly did she say?"

"She said she got sick at lunch and went home."

"It's probably the stomach flu."

"Then why did she hang up on me?"

"Dougie, you've had the stomach flu. She probably had to make a quick run to the bathroom. What was she supposed to do, explain it to you as she ran?"

"I guess I'm overreacting."

"Don't sweat it."

"I'll call her after the game, see if she's feeling better."

"You do that."

Doug managed to watch one inning before he felt himself starting to doze off.

JILL LEFT the air conditioner off and opened the car window. As she drove, the hot, humid air that rushed into her face didn't cool her off, but instead made her more miserable. Which is what she wanted. She didn't think she'd ever feel good again and, what's more, she didn't think she deserved to.

Doug. Prince Lacayo. What was the matter with her that she hadn't seen it from the start? After one look at him, she had raced through Susan's diary to see if she had mentioned him and, when she didn't find anything, wondered at her sister's stupidity. Well, it was her own stupidity she was wondering about now.

It was totally believable that Susan had been attracted to him. And it was beginning to seem just as believable that he had been attracted to Susan. After all, he'd been attracted to her when he thought she was seventeen. And sure, maybe he ran from her at first, but that was probably because of what had happened to Susan.

And that was the big question: what *had* happened to her? She no longer thought it was a childish accident. He had dated her sister secretly, just as he was now dating her. And both times the secrecy was to ensure his job, the job he claimed to hate. She was sure that many teachers had dated many students over the years, but why did it have to be her sister?

She supposed that some people would jump to the conclusion that he killed her to shut her up about it, but she didn't believe that. She refused to believe that a man who could make such tender love could also be capable of taking a young girl's life. Maybe she was being naïve, but she just didn't think it was possible that Doug was a killer.

And yet she hadn't seen any evidence of grief. He had certainly lied to her. He had discussed the suicide in class, he had made out that stupid questionnaire asking who had ever dated secretly, all the time letting her think he was helping her. If he could be that devious, maybe any behavior on his part was believable.

Trader must not have known about Susan. Surely two of them couldn't be keeping such a secret. She wondered if Doug had a history of dating students, if there was some record of it in Chicago.

Thank God for Alan. Maybe Alan would be able to give her some answers. He must know about it, else why his concern in telling her about Doug? Perhaps he had been a friend of Susan's. Perhaps she had confided in him as she had in Phaedra. Maybe it was only her family she hadn't told. That made perfect sense, because her parents would've had him arrested, and Jill would certainly have disapproved in her letters. Poor Susan. How quickly her fairy tale romance had ended in tragedy.

Jill drove into the parking lot at the beach and spotted Alan's car. As she pulled in beside it, she saw Alan and David and Mark inside.

Alan got out of the car and walked over to her window. "Good timing. We just got here."

Jill nodded her head in the direction of the other boys. "Do they have to be here?"

"They're just going to play a little ball on the beach while we talk." He opened the door for her. "Come on, let's walk along the water."

It was cooler on the beach with a breeze coming in off the ocean. Jill left her shoes in the car and walked barefoot beside Alan down to the water's edge. She saw Mark taking practice swings with a bat while David pounded a ball into his glove.

Alan put his arm around her and let his hand rest lightly on her shoulder. She didn't object. She could use an arm around her right now.

"I like you," said Alan.

"I like you, too."

"I like your intelligence. I like your sense of humor. I also like the fact that you're an older woman."

"I thought you were seventeen, Alan."

"I was eighteen last month."

"Then you're three months older than me, so what's all this older woman business? What did you want to tell me?"

"I know who you are, Jill."

"I'm just the daughter of missionaries."

"Susan used to talk about you. How you'd been in the Peace Corps and then in Africa."

She gave up any thought of denying it. In a way it was a relief that he knew. "You knew Susan?"

"We were friends."

"How did you find out about me?"

"I knew the first day. First there was your name—at least the first name. Then the fact that you were from Ethiopia. And you also look rather like her."

"I thought I fooled everyone."

"You probably did. You do a very good impersonation of a teenager at times."

"Didn't you wonder what I was doing there?"

"I figured it had to do with Susan. I was hoping you'd eventually level with me. And in the meantime I was really enjoying you as a friend. You sure make high school girls look boring in comparison."

Jill saw a jet banking over the water before heading due north. For a moment she wished she were on the plane and not here, about to hear whatever it was he was going to tell her. "What about Mr. Lacayo?" she asked.

"I think you should forget about him. He's a lightweight."

"Was she interested in him?"

"Jill, I think you're special. You're smarter than Susan. You've been around, seen things. You're probably familiar with death."

"Is he the prince?"

"Who?"

"Mr. Lacayo."

"What prince?" Alan, who seldom looked bewildered, looked it now.

"The prince Susan kept writing about in her diary."

"I didn't know she kept a diary."

"Was she seeing Mr. Lacayo secretly?"

Alan stopped and turned her to face him. "No, Jill, she was seeing *me* secretly."

"Are you sure she wasn't seeing him?"

"Very sure."

She took a step back and felt water on her foot. "Then tell me what happened to her."

Alan shrugged. "She killed herself."

Jill dug her toes into the wet sand as though to center herself. "I *know* she didn't kill herself. If she wasn't seeing Mr. Lacayo, why would she kill herself?"

Alan took her hand and turned back in the direction of the pier. "She couldn't handle it."

"You said she wasn't dating him."

"Jill, she killed herself. Trust me."

Jill pulled away her hand and speeded up her walk. Up ahead, Mark and David were approaching them. Maybe they knew something that Alan wasn't telling her.

David trotted up to them, Mark right behind him. "Is she in with us?" David asked Alan.

Alan smiled at her. "I don't know. Are you in with us, Jill?"

She looked at the three of them in frustration. "Just tell me, please, what happened to Susan."

Alan gave her a regretful look. "We let her in on our secret and she kind of lost it."

"What're you talking about? Lost what?"

"I think you'll be different, Jill," said Alan. "I think you'll understand what we're doing."

"You're going to love the power," said David, looking beautiful with the setting sun making a halo of his hair.

Jill reached out a hand to Alan's chest. "Please, Alan, just tell me the truth. Whatever it is, I can handle it."

Alan closed his hand over hers, and with his other, pointed to the pier. "See those homeless men under the pier?"

Jill looked to where he was pointing and saw a mound of what looked like rags under the pier. "What about them?"

He smiled at her. "Pick one out."

"Oh, no," she moaned.

Alan's hand tightened on hers. "We'll let you choose the sacrifice tonight. Mark, let her have the bat."

Mark held out the bat to her but she was suddenly too frightened to move even a hand. "You killed them."

"We put them out of their misery," said Alan, "and at the same time, rid society of its dregs."

She knew she should humor them, pretend to go along with them, but she just couldn't do it, not even to save herself. *"You murdered them."*

Alan sighed. "You're beginning to sound like Susan."

"You probably murdered her, too," she said, breaking away from them and running in the direction of the pier. "Run," she shouted at the people under the pier. "Run, they're going to kill you!" She heard the boys right behind her and knew she didn't have a chance, but maybe, with a little warning, she'd be the only one killed tonight.

And then, up ahead, she saw what looked like a dark cloud rising up from beneath the pier. The cloud separated, and suddenly there were men, carrying bottles and sticks and what looked like a broom, and they were coming in her direction. The homeless men, who had never tried to save themselves, were now coming to her rescue.

Jill stepped out of the way as the mass of homeless men rushed by her, then she turned and saw Alan and Mark and David racing down the beach. Being young and athletic, they'd probably outrun the men, but if she had anything to do with it, they weren't going to out race the law.

It was then that she realized for the first time that Doug was innocent. He wasn't the prince, he hadn't been involved with Susan, and he really loved her. She sank to her knees in the sand, an overwhelming feeling of relief coursing through her body.

IT WAS THE MIDDLE of the night when he heard the pounding on the door but he hadn't been asleep. He'd been too worried about Jill to sleep, too worried when he got no answer on her phone all night. Finally, a little after midnight, he'd ignored Trader's advice and driven over to her apartment. There was a light on inside but no one answered the door, and only the sight of lights going on in the main house had finally made him give up and return home. His worst fear was that she was sorry about last night and didn't want to see him again. He didn't know how that could've happened when he was so much in love with her, but he'd never pretended to understand women.

He pulled on his shorts and went to the door. He opened it to a wild-looking Jill—bedraggled, exhausted, her face tear-stained.

He pulled her in and held her close. "My God, what's the matter?"

"Just hold me for a minute, Doug," she said, burrowing her head into his shoulder and holding on to him for dear life. He knew something had happened to her. He'd kill whoever was responsible for this.

"I thought it was you," she murmured.

"What?"

"I thought you were the prince."

He tried to hold her away from him, to look her in the face, but she wouldn't let go of him. "Me? Why would you think *I* was the prince?"

"Because I was stupid," she mumbled.

"I love you," he said, "don't you know that? Don't you know how crazy I am about you?"

"That's what made it so horrible, thinking you were the prince and knowing I loved you."

"A touching scene," said Trader from the doorway of his bedroom, "but it's the middle of the night, kids."

"Leave us alone," yelled Doug, and Trader disappeared, his door slamming behind him.

"Come on in," he said to Jill, letting go of her and closing the door. "You need a drink?"

She shook her head.

He led her over to the couch and then sat down, pulling her onto his lap. She seemed to need comforting, and he loved the fact that she had come to him for it.

"This has been the worst night of my life," she said, while Doug wondered if she was referring to the flu. "I just came from the police station."

He could only give her a wordless look. Nothing that she was saying was making any sense.

"Alan, Alan and his friends, they've been killing the homeless men. He's the prince, Doug. He admitted it to me."

He smoothed her hair back from her face and said, "I think you'd better tell me the whole story."

SHE FINISHED up with, "And then I came over here. Oh, Doug, I can't believe I thought that of you, even for a moment. You must hate me for it."

"Hate you? That would be impossible. And I can see where it would all make sense. Other than the fact that I'm not attracted to seventeen-year-old girls."

"You thought I was seventeen."

"That's just it, though, you weren't. I was really attracted to a twenty-seven-year-old."

"I don't feel any better knowing the truth. I thought I would, but somehow this is even more horrible than I had imagined."

He leaned over and kissed her eyelids. "I wish I had been with you. You never should've had to go through that alone. If I had been there—"

She put her hands along the sides of his face and looked into his caring eyes. "Hush. You're not a violent sort of man at all."

"If it meant protecting you—"

"I appreciate the thought but I like to think you would have managed it all quite nonviolently. That's one thing I love about you."

He looked pleased. "What are the others?"

She managed a small smile. "You'd better take notes on this because I'm going to quiz you later."

"I don't mind being quizzed in bed."

"Is that where we're going to be later?"

He stood up, still holding her. "That's where we're going to be right now."

She put her arms around his neck, feeling a contentment she had never before felt. This is where she wanted to be now and where she'd always want to be. "Tell me again how much you love me," she said.

"I'd die for you."

She nodded. "That's exactly the way I feel about you."

"But I hope I'm not called upon to die before we've had a chance to make love."

She was smiling when he lowered her to the bed.

Epilogue

Jill walked to the door of civics and looked inside. It was five minutes before the bell, and Doug was holding forth. At one point he turned and saw her and beckoned her in. She was somewhat nervous about showing up in class suddenly as an adult, but by this time the whole school knew what had happened.

"Feel free to join the class," said Doug as she came into the room.

She felt the eyes of the students on her. She looked back at them and saw some curious looks and a few approving looks and, in the back row, four empty seats. The remaining jocks were studiously avoiding her eyes.

Jill perched on the edge of the desk next to Doug. "Mr. Lacayo thought maybe some of you would have some questions," she said.

There was silence for a moment, and then one of the girls said, "What's going to happen to them?"

"If you read the papers, you'd know," said Doug.

"Since Alan's eighteen," said Jill, "he's going to be tried as an adult. David confessed and is going to testify for the state in exchange for immunity. He will have to go to a drug and alcohol rehabilitation center, though. Mark will be tried separately as a juvenile."

One of the jocks spoke up. "We're all guilty," he mumbled.

"What?" said Jill.

He looked up at her. "We all knew Alan was seeing your sister."

"Did you also know the boys were killing the homeless men?" she asked.

The class was dead silent.

One of the girls spoke up. "There were rumors, but I don't think anyone believed them. I guess we should've done something."

"I wouldn't have believed them, either," said Jill. "Alan had me fooled, too."

"Did he kill your sister?" asked one of the boys.

"That's what David claims. I guess it will be up to the jury to decide."

The bell rang but no one moved. Doug finally had to say, "Hey, get out of here. And do me a favor and read the paper tonight."

The class filed out quietly; a couple of the girls stopping to tell Jill how sorry they were about Susan. When they were all out, Doug closed the door.

"That was tougher than coming in here pretending to be a teenager," said Jill.

"You did great."

"I was afraid I might cry."

"You? No way. You're too tough for that." He put his arms around her and pulled her close. "Come on, I've got the rest of the day off, and we're driving down to the Keys for the weekend."

"I have to see one more person. I want to say goodbye to Phaedra."

"Do you know where she is this period?"

"Study hall."

"Wait right here and I'll get her out of there."

Jill sat down behind Doug's desk. It seemed strange being in the front of the room instead of in the back row. In a couple of minutes, Phaedra walked into the classroom alone.

"Hi," said Jill.

Phaedra burst into tears.

Jill got up and went around the desk. She tried to put her arms around the girl, but Phaedra backed away.

"Don't touch me," wailed Phaedra.

"I'm sorry. I didn't like having to lie to you."

Phaedra's eyes grew startled. "You don't have anything to be sorry about. I should've been honest with you, but I wanted you for a friend."

"You knew about Alan?"

"No, I would've told you if I had known that. It's you I knew about. I knew you were her sister."

"And here I thought I was fooling everybody."

"She told me all about you. She was always talking about you."

"Phaedra, that's okay. I appreciated having you as a friend, too."

"Really?"

"Really. And I loved going to the dance with you."

"I'm going to miss you, Jill."

"Maybe you could write to me. Tell me what's happening."

"I'd love to write to you," said Phaedra, the crying coming to a halt. "I know it won't be the same as Susan writing to you."

"No, it won't be a sister, but it'll be a friend."

Jill saw Doug standing in the doorway. Phaedra saw him, too, and started to grin.

"I *knew* you had a crush on him," said Phaedra.

Doug was looking awfully pleased at the news.

"I have more than a crush," said Jill. "We're going to be married."

"Are you really?" asked Phaedra, a smile suddenly lighting up her face. "When?"

"Yes, when?" asked Doug, coming into the room. "I don't recall proposing yet."

"Well, you would've waited so long," said Jill.

"I was going to propose this weekend. In a romantic setting."

"What could be more romantic than here, where we met?" Jill asked him, knowing that their conversation was delighting Phaedra.

Doug glanced over at Phaedra then back at Jill. "I kind of wanted to be alone with you when I did it."

"Don't be shy," said Jill. "Prove to Phaedra that there are happy endings."

"Why don't we invite Woleski in to hear it, too," said Doug, but he was looking amused.

"Good idea," said Jill. "Phaedra, go get Mr. Woleski out of his class and tell him to come here."

Phaedra looked to Doug for approval, and when he nodded, she rushed to the door. She turned back to say, "Don't do anything until I get back."

"We won't," Jill assured her.

When she was gone, Doug said, "Oh, yes we will," and took her into his arms. The kiss was long and sweet, and when it ended he said, "Maybe we should call an assembly and announce it in the auditorium."

"Just because we're in civics doesn't mean we have to argue," said Jill, lifting her mouth again for his kiss. While arguing with Doug was fun, this was even better.

H A R L E Q U I N
American Romance®

COMING NEXT MONTH

#333 SIGHT UNSEEN by Kathy Clark

It wasn't a whimsical flight of fancy that stable owner Nicki Chandler reported to detective Jake Kelly. Nicki had been visited by a series of waking dreams—dreams she was convinced mirrored a real-life tragedy. Jake never expected that Nicki's dreams held danger—and a direct challenge to a new and fragile love.

Don't miss the second book in the ROCKY MOUNTAIN MAGIC series.

#334 MEANT TO BE by Cathy Gillen Thacker

He was a man with everything—everything but a family. Tom Harrigan, the eldest son in the prominent Harrigan clan, had always won his heart's desire. But now, the surrogate mother of his baby son threatened to destroy his dreams. Cynthia Whittiker, the attractive court-appointed guardian, showed him that love was never a game of lose or win.

#335 NIGHTSHADE by Ginger Chambers

Christian Townsend was rich, handsome, self-assured and smart, and museum employee Sonya Douglas didn't know how she was going to manage him. When Christian probed the unsolved theft of priceless artifacts, he brought the museum close to scandal. But when Sonya finally succeeded in dividing his interest—which then focused on her—the situation got totally out of control.

#336 TALL COTTON by Lori Copeland

Kelly Smith had always planned to follow in her father's footsteps on the horse-racing circuit, but now it seemed those footsteps led to betrayal. Could she prove her father had been innocent of the charges against him? She'd been forced to deceive Tanner McCrey, the man behind the accusations, to find out whether he was ally or enemy. Now would she ever be able to win his love?

THE STANLEY HOTEL—
A HISTORY

Upon moving to Colorado, F. O. Stanley fell in love with Estes Park, a town nestled in an alpine mountain bowl at 7,500 feet, the Colorado Rockies towering around it.

With an initial investment of $500,000, Stanley designed and began construction of The Stanley Hotel in 1906. Materials and supplies were transported 22 miles by horse teams on roads constructed solely for this purpose. The grand opening took place in 1909 and guests were transported to The Stanley Hotel in steam-powered, 12-passenger "mountain wagons" that were also designed and built by Stanley.

On May 26, 1977, The Stanley Hotel was entered in the National Register of Historic Places and is still considered by many as one of the significant factors contributing to the growth of Colorado as a tourist destination.

We hope you enjoy visiting The Stanley Hotel in our "Rocky Mountain Magic" series in American Romance.

RMH-1